THE DAY HE CAME HOME

HAWTHORNE HARBOR SECOND CHANCE
ROMANCE, BOOK 5

ELANA JOHNSON

AEJ
CREATIVE WORKS

ISBN-13: 978-1-953506-08-5

1

———

Hunter Magleby watched the ocean on his left-hand side, his heart slowly sinking toward his feet with every mile that passed. Well, the left one at least could still feel something. His right foot ached with a numbness the doctors said would probably never go away.

Sure, some days were better than others, and Hunter tried to keep his thoughts on the positive.

I'm still alive.

I have somewhere to live.

I got an honorable discharge from the Marines.

"Have you been to Hawthorne Harbor?" his driver asked, breaking into Hunter's thoughts.

"Yes," he said without looking away from the ocean. It was beautiful, and he hadn't realized how much he'd missed the sight of it, the smell of it, the constant way it drove toward the shore.

He finally tore his eyes from the water and looked out the windshield. "I grew up there, actually."

"Oh, is your family still here?" The driver was asking to be conversational, Hunter knew. People everywhere seemed to be extra kind to him, and he knew it was because of the uniform he wore and the cane he used. Otherwise, they probably wouldn't even look in his direction.

His anxiety tripled when he thought about how his great aunt would receive him, but he pushed it back. After all, Hunter had a ton of experience in burying emotions and getting the job done. And that was what he needed to do in Hawthorne Harbor.

"No," he said. "Well, sort of. My parents moved when I joined the Marines. But there are plenty of Maglebys still in Hawthorne Harbor." Too many, actually, but Hunter kept that info under his tongue. He was looking forward to seeing Aunt Mabel, and she'd told him that Lauren lived just down the hill from the Mansion.

In fact, it would be his cousin Lauren who'd fixed up the house where he'd be living, and he had a gift for her in his backpack.

The driver stopped talking then, and Hunter leaned back into the seat behind him, almost hoping time would slow enough to stop. Then he wouldn't have to return to a town that had forgotten him. He wouldn't have to face the past he'd left behind. He wouldn't have to try to figure out who he was now that he wasn't a soldier.

A sigh gathered in his chest, but he kept it contained. Another skill he'd picked up from the numerous meetings he'd endured over the years. He could keep his face completely passive for long periods of time too, and he never, *ever* let his emotions show if he didn't want them to.

He felt like he'd been living behind a slab of stone since the accident that had stolen his mobility from him. Stolen his career.

You're still alive, he started mentally reciting again. You have a good place to live. Family nearby to help. Money coming in.

The road curved, and the ocean moved behind them. The outskirts of town appeared, and Hunter steeled himself to step back in time.

The driver took him right to the house on the northwest side of town, just down from the bluff. He jumped out of the car to get Hunter's bags, and Hunter took his time getting out of the back seat and positioning his cane to help balance himself.

"There he is." Lauren came down the front steps, a smile on her face. She didn't even look at his leg or the angry pink scar clawing up from underneath his collar. Her long, dark hair bounced along her shoulders, and a man Hunter didn't recognize followed her. He took Lauren's hand as they approached, and Hunter's wariness returned. He hadn't realized he'd have a whole welcoming committee.

Lauren let go of her boyfriend's hand and embraced Hunter. "You look great."

Ah, so his cousin was a liar now. Hunter smiled anyway. "Thanks. How long have you been back in town?" Her family had left like his, and it was almost an unwritten rule that Magleby's didn't live anywhere but Hawthorne Harbor.

"About seven years," she said. "This is Trent Baker, my husband."

"Oh, congrats," Hunter said, leaning all of his weight on his left leg so he could extend his right hand to Trent.

"Nice to meet you," Trent said, a smile on his face that disappeared quickly.

"Are you Army?" he asked Trent.

"No." Trent shook his head. "I used to be a cop, but now I train dogs to be police animals."

"Ah." So he was in a similar field of work as Hunter. He could always spot those who had some sort of experience dealing with difficult situations, and cops made great soldiers.

"So your place is properly aired out and ready for you," Lauren said, stepping toward the front porch, where the driver had set Hunter's bags. "Trent, Porter, and I live just down the road. Aunt Mabel is bringing her apple twist bread by later."

"She doesn't have to do that," Hunter said, looking at the eight steps that led up to the house. The thought of climbing up and down these every day made his muscles tighten and his brain tell him to find somewhere else to live.

"I know," Lauren said. "But she insisted, and you know how Aunt Mabel can be."

"Pushy?" Hunter said, which caused both Trent and Lauren to laugh. Neither of them reached to help him, which he appreciated. They also didn't walk slower because of him or wait for him. They just went up the steps and into the house, and when Hunter got there, he found three dogs sitting nicely beside Trent.

"This is our welcome home gift to you," Lauren said, beaming down at the canines.

"A dog?" Hunter asked.

"Not just a dog," Trent said. "A trained service animal. They can do all kinds of things."

Hunter blinked, his first reaction to decline a service animal. He wasn't disabled. He didn't need help. But in the back of his mind and way down deep in his heart, he knew he was disabled, and he did need help.

"Like what?" he asked.

Trent exchanged a glance with Lauren that didn't go unnoticed by Hunter. "You balance on the couch and hand me your cane." Trent strode forward and took it from Hunter. He put it on the table behind him and whistled at the dogs. All three of them shifted toward him, and one of them whined.

"Sh," Trent said, and the dog quieted immediately.

"You give him a command to get the cane, and he will." Trent pointed to it and said, "Geronimo, get it."

The big German shepherd took a few steps and put his front paws up on the table. He scrabbled around for a moment, finally getting the cane in his jaws and backing up and dropping back to all fours.

"You tell him to bring it," Trent said.

"Bring it," Hunter barked, and the dog trotted toward him, tilted his head back, and let Hunter take the cane from his hand.

"You can tell him to drop it," Trent said. "He can get almost anything you want him to. Geronimo is the one I'd pick for you." He glanced at the other two dogs. "But Clara is great too, and she really likes to cuddle during downtime. If you like that...." He let his words die there, and Lauren took over.

"Have her open the door," she said.

"You want to see her do that?" Trent didn't wait for Hunter to answer. He walked to the front door while he talked. "I'll go out and ring the doorbell. You tell her to answer. Just like that. 'Answer it, Clara,' and she will."

He ducked outside and closed the door behind him. A moment later the doorbell rang. All three dogs turned toward it, and Hunter said, "Answer it, Clara."

The smaller golden retriever trotted over to the door and jumped up. With her front paws on either side of the handle, she used her chin to push it down. As she backed up, the door drifted open to reveal a very proud Trent standing there.

Hunter had no idea what to say or do. He knew the dogs made him happy, and he couldn't help smiling. "They're great, Trent. They must cost a lot of money."

"Loads," Lauren said. "So which one do you want?"

He looked at the German shepherd who'd brought him his cane, and the pretty golden retriever who'd opened the door. The third dog had laid down at Lauren's feet, his tongue hanging out of his mouth.

"I like Clara."

"She's yours," Trent said, stooping to scrub down the pup. "He chose you, you lucky girl. Yes, you're so lucky. He wants you."

She grinned up at him and took his praise and affection, and Hunter decided that being back in Hawthorne Harbor wasn't so bad if he could have that pretty dog at his side—and Lauren and Trent just down the street.

THE NEXT DAY, LAUREN PULLED UP TO THE HOSPITAL, AND Hunter said, "I really can go in myself," after she'd offered to accompany him inside.

"All right." She grinned easily at him. "Text me when you're done. I'm on a job site only a block away, and I'll come get you."

"I can probably get a ride." He unbuckled his seatbelt

and opened the door, the autumn wind practically ripping the door off its hinges.

"Really?" Lauren asked. "With who?" At least she wasn't afraid of offending him.

"I don't know," he mumbled.

"Text me."

"Fine." He slid out of her truck, it being much easier to get to his feet from a taller vehicle. He leaned into his cane and limped into the hospital, still twenty minutes early for his appointment.

Still plenty of time, he coached himself. Lots of sick people in the hospital. Hardly anyone glanced his way. You can walk. You're alive.

He kept up the positive self-talk all the way to the elevator and up to the third floor of the hospital, where the physical therapy unit was located. He was sure they'd put it in the farthest corner of the hospital as some sort of sick joke.

An atrium sat on his right, and the hallway beside that led down to the children's wing. A few people sat on the benches with the plants surrounding them, eating lunch. He watched them for a moment, a smile coursing through his body and crossing his face.

A woman eating with a boy sat in the corner, and Hunter's eyes caught on them. She lifted her head, her dark, wavy hair falling over her shoulders and that oh-so-familiar smile lighting up her face as she laughed.

Alice.

Hunter's breath caught in his lungs, and he choked. Plenty of people around to help with that, but he knew he didn't need physical help.

Of course he'd run into Alice Kopp. Her family were Hawthorne Harbor natives, same as his. And he'd left her here when he'd answered his summons to enter active duty, nine years ago.

His wife.

Well, ex-wife now. That marriage had only lasted seven days before Alice had gotten it annulled. Hunter had been notified first by her and then by the court, and he'd never heard from Alice again.

But that woman was definitely her. He'd know her anywhere, as she'd been the first woman he'd fallen in love with. They'd gotten married spontaneously, sure. Irrationally, even. But Hunter had thought they could make it work.

He loved her. She loved him. That was enough, wasn't it?

Apparently not, and one of the main reasons he hadn't come back to Hawthorne Harbor before now was sitting twenty feet from him.

Alice wore a pair of pale pink scrubs, which meant she obviously worked here, and the child she was with was probably seven or eight years old. Probably a patient, but Hunter watched as Alice checked her watch, said something to the boy, and leaned over to hug him.

They got up together and started toward him. Hunter

panicked, everything in him telling him to move. Get out of the way. Disappear somehow.

Because Alice was going to see him.

Before he could even get his good leg to take a step, she looked up and right into his eyes. She froze.

He was already cemented in place. Behind him, the elevator dinged, and he thought maybe he could just fall backward and the car doors would swoop closed, concealing him.

The boy took a few more steps before turning back and saying, "Mom?"

Mom, Mom, Mom.

The word echoed endlessly in Hunter's head. So Alice had indeed moved on. Found someone else to marry. Had a kid now.

"Well," a woman said, and Hunter managed to turn to look at her. Alice's mother. She hadn't been terribly supportive of Hunter and Alice's youthful romance, nor their shotgun wedding.

"Westin," Alice said, coming up beside the boy quickly. Her voice rang every bell in Hunter's system, and he hoped for a moment that they might have another chance. After all, she'd named her son after his father.

Probably a coincidence, he thought. He couldn't even remember her mother's name at the moment. Or his. *She's married with a kid,* he told himself as he tried to find something solid to grab onto. *And you're a lame war veteran without a job or a purpose.*

Her eyes widened, and she swallowed, clearly nervous to be face-to-face with Hunter. He wondered if she felt like she was seeing a ghost, the way he did.

"Isn't this just one big family reunion?" her mother asked, her tone slightly acidic.

"Family reunion?" Hunter repeated, looking at the older woman, who had pure white hair now—something that didn't exist in his memory.

Karen—he was honestly shocked he remembered Alice's mother's name—turned to her daughter. "You didn't tell him? You *promised* me you'd told him."

Alice put her arm protectively around the boy, and Hunter's synapses were firing like cannons. He put all the pieces together quickly, always good at puzzles.

Westin had gray eyes—like his.

Westin had his mother's dark hair, but Hunter's sloped nose and square jaw.

"Westin," Alice said, her voice much higher than it had just been. "This is your father, Hunter Magleby."

Hunter felt like he was falling. Falling forever, the way he'd been when his ship had been targeted. The world spun, and he flung his arm out, trying to find something to hold onto.

"Hunter," Alice said, grounding him as she caught hold of his hand, centering him, the way she always had. "Um, this is your son, Westin. Westin Hunter Magleby."

2

Alice Kopp avoided looking at her mother. Or her son. No, she kept her eyes glued to Hunter Magleby, the ghost of a man she'd refused to let go of despite the gulf she'd placed between them.

She slipped her hand out of his as fury roared into Hunter's expression. She put both hands on her son's shoulders, hoping to use him to steady herself. Everything around her felt like it was rocking back and forth. Shaking. Maybe they were having an earthquake right now.

Or maybe all that trembling and breaking and splitting was just happening inside Alice.

"Say something," she said to Hunter, who just stood there, his weight on his cane and his dark eyes storming in a way she'd never seen before. Hunter experienced emotions deeply, she knew that.

They'd fallen in love in a single summer, and the joy

he could broadcast from his eyes was like beholding heaven.

Unfortunately, his anger and stubborn streak ran just as deeply, as she was being reminded now as she stood in front of him. The silent soldier she'd been thinking about for years. And years.

"Alice," her mother said, finally drawing her attention. Alice didn't want to deal with her mother's wrath and disappointment right now either. Her lunch break was minutes from ending, and then she'd have to get back to work.

Her heart felt like someone had tethered it to a live wire, and electricity was zinging it every few seconds.

She looked into her mother's brown eyes, so much like her own, and back to Hunter. "She needs to take Westin, Hunter."

"Maybe he can take me," Westin said, surprising Alice.

"What?" she asked at the same time her mom said, "No, Westin."

"Why not?" Westin and Hunter asked at the same time, further baffling Alice.

"He's clearly here for an appointment," her mother said, looking at Hunter.

"I could go with him." Westin turned and faced Alice. "Right, Mom?"

Alice looked into her son's eyes, so much like his father's. Her heart constricted, and she didn't want to deny him anything.

"How old are you?" Hunter asked, and Westin spun back to him.

"Eight," Westin said. "I'll be nine in March."

"A few months," Alice said, watching Hunter as he did the math. Would he ask for a paternity test? Couldn't he see himself in his son? Alice certainly could, and sometimes she wondered why she'd never said anything to Hunter about the baby. Then the toddler. The little boy. The child.

Deep down, she knew why. She wanted Hunter Magleby to return to Hawthorne Harbor of his own accord, not because she'd drawn him back against his will. A part of her wanted him to return to town for her, too, not because he had to.

But because he *wanted* to.

However, it didn't take her nursing degree to see that Hunter didn't want to be here.

"I do have an appointment in a couple of minutes," he said, his voice softer than it had been a moment ago. He bent down to look into Westin's face. "And they're long, so you can't really come with me."

"But—"

"But we'll see each other again soon."

"Promise?" Westin asked, and Alice's heart folded itself into a tiny box. She knew what it was like to make a promise to her son and then have to break it. She didn't want him to get hurt by Hunter, and immediate guilt flooded her. *She* was the one who hadn't told him about his son. Hadn't given him the opportunity to be a father for eight, long years.

"Of course," he said, straightening. Pain flashed across his face, and Alice's keen nurse's eyes saw it all. His gaze bored into hers, all that fury and frustration returning in a single heartbeat. "I'll call you." Without another word, he turned and limped down the hall toward the physical therapy unit, somehow an angry stomp in his steps even with his injury.

"Go on, Westin," she said, her voice barely more than a whisper and her eyes refusing to let go of Hunter's broad shoulders and long legs.

"Come on, baby," her mom said, gathering Westin into her body. She also met Alice's eyes, and Alice sure hoped someone would look at her with less than contempt that day. "I can't believe you." She shook her head, curled one arm around her grandson, and guided him to the elevator.

Alice felt like someone had filled her veins with ice water, and she rubbed her hands up and down her arms as if cold. Realizing she was late, she hurried back to her station and signed in.

"Who was the handsome man you were talking to out there?" Sadie Benjamin picked up her soda and took a long drink.

"Do you have one of those for me?" Alice sighed and rubbed her forehead though she still had six hours left in her shift.

Sadie nodded toward a Styrofoam cup with a bright

red straw. Relief spread through Alice, and she reached for the drink.

"Oh, he must be someone special," Sadie said.

Alice almost choked on the cold diet cola, the carbonation burning her throat in all the best ways. She sighed again and looked back the way she'd come, though the atrium was down two hallways and couldn't be seen.

"That was Hunter Magleby."

Sadie wasn't from Hawthorne Harbor, but she'd heard enough stories about Westin's father to know to gasp, eyes wide, and cover her mouth with her hand. "You're kidding? He's back in town? Did you know he was back in town?"

"I did not," Alice said, picking up a chart she needed to read. The letters blurred, and she couldn't focus at all.

"And you told him about Westin?"

"I had to. My mother showed up and started throwing around words like *family reunion*." She took another drink of her soda, hoping the caffeine would jumpstart her brain into thinking properly. She started to move out from behind the desk when Sadie stepped in front of her.

"But you would've told him anyway, right?" Sadie looked down at her, and Alice wished she wasn't always looking up into people's faces. "Right, Alice? I mean, Westin is *his son*."

"I know who Westin is," she said, so exhausted she could drop onto a cot in the dark room and sleep for hours. Well, probably not. Her mind would probably circle and obsess and never let her drift off.

No one understood why she hadn't told Hunter about Westin. Alice wasn't sure she understood it either. But no one understood Hunter the way she did. No one knew him the way she did.

Which is all the more reason why you should've told him, she lectured herself. Because she did know he'd be furious. And he wouldn't call. He'd find out where she lived, and he'd stop by her house. Heck, he'd probably be waiting on her front porch when she got home.

"So now what?" Sadie asked, running her fingers through her wavy, blonde hair.

"He's going to call me," she said. "But I'm going to try to catch him after his physical therapy appointment."

"Physical therapy?"

"He was walking with a cane." Concern ran through her, making her heart skip one beat, then two. He'd been injured in his service overseas—exactly as she'd feared he would. Alice didn't want to get into all of her weaknesses today, so she pushed against the emotions rising through her and squinted at the chart.

"Okay, I'm off to little Teddy's room."

"I was just in there," Angela Harding, another nurse, said as she approached the nurse's station. "I gave him the meds. I'll note it." She plucked the chart from Alice's hands with a smile. She scratched a note onto the chart and handed it back to Alice. "Okay, what did I interrupt?"

"Nothing," Alice said, shooting at glance at Sadie.

"Her ex is back in town. Westin's dad. Has a cane and is going to physical therapy."

Ang blinked a few times as she took in all that information. Alice wanted the floor to open up and swallow her whole. Ang's green eyes seemed to draw secrets right out of Alice.

"So we're going for hot chocolate after work," she said.

"I can't," Alice said immediately, thinking of Hunter out in the cold Washington January, waiting for her and Westin to come home.

"Oh, yes, you can." Ang reached over the counter and picked up her phone. "I'll text your mom right now."

"Ang," Alice warned.

"Come on," Sadie said, looping her arm through Alice's. "Come check on the baby twins with me."

"Oh, that's not fair," Alice said, walking away with Sadie but watching Ang over her shoulder. She loved the twin boys who'd been born premature and had spent the first seven weeks of their life in her wing. She loved holding one or both of them during her graveyard shift as they ate. Loved the baby soft feel of their skin. The baby powder scent of their hair and clothes.

But today, even the twin babies couldn't distract her from the thought of coming face-to-face with Hunter again.

AFTER AN HOUR AT THE HOT CHOCOLATE BAR, AND AFTER she'd asked her mom to keep Westin for a little longer, Alice drove slowly down the dirt road that led to one of the Magleby houses. Specifically, the one Hunter had moved into a couple of days ago.

Her headlights cut through the darkness, and she flexed her fingers on the steering wheel. A pit in her stomach told her this was a very bad idea. Hunter had never liked surprises—at least when he was on the receiving end. He loved giving surprises, and the biggest one of all had come when he'd announced he'd joined the Marines after they'd been dating for a couple of months.

The engine idled while she peered at the house on Forgotten Road. It looked more like a log cabin than a house, but it fit in perfectly with all the trees, bushes, and undeveloped land surrounding it. The Magleby Mansion sat on the bluff above the house, and the family owned all the land surrounding it, including the hills, and several houses on this lane and across the highway.

Alice didn't care about any of those houses. She just cared about this one. And not even the house, but the man inside it.

"Go on," she whispered to herself. She'd made the arrangements with Westin so she could talk to Hunter alone. She'd been right; he hadn't called. Maybe he wasn't as resourceful as he'd once been. He'd matured since they'd met at the Lavender Festival in high school. His shoulders had filled out, and his hair had carried a hint of gray when she'd seen him in the hospital.

His thirty-first birthday had come and gone last fall, so he wasn't that old, but he'd definitely had silver hair. He could hide it if he wanted to—the Hunter she'd known and loved could do anything he wanted. He'd asked around until he'd found someone who would give him her phone number, and he'd kept it in his pocket for weeks before calling her.

So why hadn't he called today?

Horrible, traitorous thoughts about how he didn't want to see Westin paraded through her mind.

Please don't let that be it, she prayed as she got out of the car. Her feet ached after her long shift in the children's ward, but she'd endured worse pain. She climbed the steps and employed every ounce of bravery she possessed to knock on the door.

She leaned close to the wood, trying to hear anything behind it.

"Answer it, Clara," she heard, and her pulse bounced like a basketball. Hunter was home, but she had no idea who Clara was. Alice almost bolted. It was dark. He didn't know her car. She didn't know any Clara's, and she was a Hawthorne Harbor native.

Maybe he'd gotten married while he served in the Marines. Maybe that was why he hadn't called. Why he didn't want Westin in his life.

Scratching sounded against the door, and in the next

moment, it opened. It slowly drifted inward, and she saw a beautiful golden retriever sitting there.

"Come, Clara," Hunter said, and the dog immediately trotted over to where he sat in an armchair next to the fireplace. A beat passed, and then he added, "You might as well come in too. It's cold out there."

Alice felt the sting of his words all the way down in her toes. The only reason he wanted her to come in was to keep out the cold. *Doesn't matter*, she told herself as she entered and closed the door.

"Hello, Hunter. Your dog can open the door?"

He simply looked at her, his fingers stroking his retriever slowly. Alice rubbed her hands together and looked around the house. Definitely more of a cabin, with red and blue checkered curtains above the windows and black bear figurines on the mantel.

"Do you even want to see Westin?" she asked, deciding to get right to the point.

"Of course I do," Hunter said, his voice soft but not concealing the undercurrent of anger there. He rose slowly, balancing himself with the armrests of the chair. He stood at his full height, his gaze filled with lasers. "I can't believe we have a child, and you didn't tell me."

Everything inside Alice quivered. Tears sprang to her eyes. She couldn't speak past the huge lump in her throat.

"I'm so angry with you," he said, his quiet fury worse than if he'd yelled. Hunter said so few things, that what he did vocalize actually meant something.

"I know," she said, the tears in her voice as they splashed her face. "I'm sorry, Hunter. I'm so sorry."

He pressed his right hand against his thigh and stepped first with that leg. In stuttering and yet graceful movement, he limped over to the door, giving her a wide berth. "I'd like to take him to breakfast in the morning."

"That's fine," she said. "I usually work graveyards, and he stays with my parents. I was just on the day shift for today, because I have the weekend off."

Hunter opened the door and held onto it tightly. "Is nine o'clock too early?"

"No," she said, wondering if she'd ever feel normal again now that Hunter was back. If she was being completely honest with herself, she hadn't felt normal since he'd left. Her pregnancy hadn't been particularly easy, and she'd lived with the constant fear that Hunter would never return to Hawthorne Harbor. She wasn't sure if she'd worried more about that or if the fact that he could come back had eaten at her more.

No matter what, the last nine years of Alice's life had been a constant roller coaster for her emotions.

"I'll pick him up then. At your mother's?"

"I have my own place."

He reached into his pocket and withdrew a slip of paper. "Text me the address." He extended the paper to her, and she took it, this conversation clearly over.

She moved to go outside, pausing close to him. Too close. Close enough to smell his cologne and see the flecks of blue in those stormy gray eyes. "I'm really am sorry."

He nodded once, his jaw hard and square. He looked somewhere past her, and Alice didn't know what else to do. She'd imagined the moment she'd tell Hunter about Westin, and it had never happened in the hospital atrium.

He had been angry with her, but he'd forgiven her so quickly. She had whole speeches prepared, but all of those words had fled as soon as she'd seen his face. She certainly couldn't spill all her irrational reasons for why she'd never said anything about Westin.

She stretched up on her toes and swept her lips across his cheek. Horrified at what she'd done—eight years ago and now—she scampered out the door and down the steps, leaving Hunter inside his cabin and wishing her heart didn't still beat with excitement at the mere thought of him. And being in the same space? An exquisite kind of torture she wanted to repeat as soon as possible.

3

Hunter stood very still, the sweet smell of Alice still lingering in his nose and the heat from her lips against his cheek like a brand. Clara came over and laid against his feet, putting pressure against his right leg he couldn't take.

"Move, Clara," he said as gently as he could with the hurricane in his whole soul. The dog got up and moved, thankfully, and he gritted his teeth as he hobbled back to the armchair. He shouldn't have gotten up and walked without his cane, even to prove a point. Especially to Alice, of all people. He didn't have anything to prove to her.

And yet, he wanted her to know he was okay. That he didn't need her pity. That he could take care of himself *and* their son.

He groaned as he settled into the chair, happy to have

Clara on his cold toes now. She laid on the floor with a soft sigh, and Hunter said, "I know, sweetheart. But you did so good answering the door."

She lifted her head as if she'd get the chance to bump down that knob again, but she didn't move. She wouldn't until he gave her the command. And right now, he could barely sit without moaning in pain.

He reached for the water bottle on the table next to him and took a shaky drink. The agony would pass, he knew. He just needed to hold very still for a few minutes. Take some deep breaths. While he did that, the burning sensation and prickly feeling in his leg diminished, but his brain reminded him that he couldn't drive.

How in the world was he going to drive to Alice's house, pick up his son, and take them to breakfast?

He let his eyes drift closed, feeling the weight of the world descend on him.

It's just a leg, he thought. I'm alive. Living in this great house.

"And I have a son." His eyes opened, and it was like he was seeing his whole life for the first time. He had a son.

He'd had the knowledge for twelve hours now, and he was still trying to wrap his mind around it. He wondered if he'd had done things differently had he known. Would he have quit the Marines earlier? Come home? Made a family with Alice and Westin?

Could he still do that?

He shook his head to clear the fantasies. Alice had

been lying to him for nine years. Nine. *Years.* He couldn't just forgive that because she'd apologized a couple of times, cried a few tears, and kissed him.

His phone buzzed, and he picked it up from the armrest. *This is Alice. My address is 3752 Champagne Avenue.*

Hunter needed to figure out a way to get there by nine o'clock. Instead of answering Alice, he sent a quick message to Lauren, asking her if she could at least drive them to the diner. Then perhaps Alice or her mother could come pick them up.

Drive him home afterward.

Humiliation filled his throat, but he swallowed it back. He'd been told he'd have to rely on other people some-times. He'd almost accepted it. But getting a ride from his cousin was completely different than asking his ex-wife— who had concealed his son from him for almost a decade —for anything. Anything at all.

The fire of anger licked inside him, and that was a feeling he was well-acquainted with. He let it burn through him for a few moments, finally capping it when he received a response from Lauren.

I can't drive you tomorrow, she said. Trent and I went to Seattle for the weekend, remember?

Hunter sighed this time, the sound a long hiss that seemed to fill the whole world. Clara lifted her head and looked at him, but he shook his head at her. Trent had told Hunter to sit on the couch and let the dog lie next to him.

He grunted through the pain and got up to move over to the couch. Once settled, he said, "Come on, Clara."

The dog leapt lightly onto the couch and came over next to him, laying down right beside him, leaning her weight comfortably into him. Peace flowed through him at the simple touch of the canine. At how much she loved him already, after only a couple of days.

He'd felt the same way about Alice once. They'd met in high school, but they hadn't started dating until a year after that. He'd drifted for a year, trying to figure out what to do with his life, and she was going to community college about thirty minutes from Hawthorne Harbor.

They'd reconnected at the Spring Fling, and she'd swept him off his feet, literally. The next couple of months had been some of the best of his life, and under the golden summer sun, he'd fallen hard and fast for Alice Kopp.

He'd also decided to enlist in the Marines, and when he'd learned he had to leave by September, he'd bought the most expensive ring he could afford at the time— which was pathetic, he knew—and proposed to the woman he loved.

Her parents had not been happy. They had not approved. But Alice had loved him. He'd loved her. They'd gotten married on the beach with the Magleby Mansion on the bluff above them, and Aunt Mabel had given them the dinner and reception following it.

They went to Victoria Island for two days for a honeymoon, and then he'd left Hawthorne Harbor. A week after that, his marriage had been annulled.

Hunter still wasn't sure where things had derailed. What he'd done wrong. Okay, he knew he'd done a lot wrong. Perhaps he should've finished his basic training and come back to town, found out if Alice still loved him, if her parents would give their blessing.

He shook his head. He couldn't dwell on decade-old decisions. He couldn't change them now. Obsessing over them and wishing to go back in time would only drive him insane, one iota at a time.

And right now, he needed to figure out how he could get himself and his son to the diner for breakfast.

Maybe ask Aunt Mabel? Lauren's next text helped him focus.

Hunter scoffed at the suggestion. Aunt Mabel had to be edging closer and closer to ninety years old, and there was no way she should be driving. *Does she drive?* he texted back.

No, but she has a driver, and if Jaime isn't doing anything, she's already paying him.

Hunter wasn't sure he wanted to be chauffeured around by a stranger, but he figured it would be better than his elderly aunt. So he texted her too, wondering if the woman even knew how to use the technology.

Her response came faster than Lauren's, and she said, Hunter Magleby. Do you know what time it is? You're asking me for a ride to breakfast? It's almost midnight.

It was still a couple of hours from midnight, but Hunter still felt the need to explain further. *I have to go*, he tapped out. *And I can't drive. Lauren's in Seattle.* Before he could send the message, another from Aunt Mabel came in.

And you should be ashamed of yourself asking me anyway. You haven't even been up to say hello yet. Back in town for two days and I haven't even gotten a hug.

Hunter smiled at the screen, a strange tingling in his eyes. Aunt Mabel was deadly serious. She wanted him to come visit her, and he didn't have to imagine how lonely she probably was.

But yesterday didn't really count as a day. Sure, he'd arrived, gotten his dog, and managed to unpack everything he owned. Honestly, that wasn't hard, as he'd learned to keep only the most essential items over the past nine years as he served in the Marines. Lauren had said Aunt Mabel would bring something by, but she never had.

And today...Today had been extremely difficult, both physically and emotionally. He was worn right to the bone, and he couldn't type all of it out in a text.

He said, I know. I'd love to come see you tomorrow. After breakfast. I have to pick someone up at nine o'clock.

Like lightning, a thought struck him. Did Aunt Mabel know about Westin? She knew everything that happened in this town—surely she'd known about Alice Kopp's pregnancy and her son.

I'm going with Westin, he added to the text and sent it. Did you know about Westin, Aunt Mabel?

Nine o'clock?

I have to be at his place at nine.

I'll be there at 8:45.

So, yes, she knew about his son. Probably everyone in town did. Why hadn't anyone said anything? Was it some Hawthorne Harbor pact they'd all made? His fury flamed again, and this time closing his eyes and taking a drink did nothing to quench the way it burned through his veins like wildfire.

"THIS IS IT," HE SAID TO JAIME, WHO DROVE THE LONG, black luxury car. Aunt Mabel rode in the front seat with him, and Hunter had the back to himself. At least for another minute.

Jaime pulled into the appointed house—a two-story home with blue siding and a bright yellow door. It screamed Alice to him, and sure enough, that sunny front door opened a moment later to reveal the dark-haired beauty that had captured his heart so quickly. She leaned in the doorway as Westin skipped down the steps wearing a pair of jeans and a black jacket zipped all the way up.

Hunter saw the softness in her eyes as she watched her son. He felt the same love in his heart, and he didn't even know the boy. *Yet*, he told himself. He didn't know him yet. But Hunter had nothing but time in front of him, and he would do whatever he could for his son—including getting out of the car when he really just wanted to stay put.

"Hey, bud," he said to the boy as he drew nearer.

"Hey, Dad." Westin came right over to him like they'd been best friends since the boy's birth. He put his arms around Hunter and hugged him. "Mom said we're going to The Bakery for breakfast."

"That's right," he said. "But we can go anywhere you want." Hunter bent down and looked into his son's face. He tried to memorize the profile, the slope of his nose, the color of his eyes, so much like looking into a mirror. "Do you want to go somewhere else?"

"No, I love the chocolate chip cookie dough pancakes at The Bakery. They're my favorite."

Hunter chuckled and held onto the door to balance himself. "Well, get in then. Those are my favorite too."

Westin said, "Really?" as he dove into the car, and Hunter wanted to turn away from Alice still framed in the doorway and continue the conversation with his son. But something made him look up to her and pause.

She still wore that soft expression, but when she found him looking at her, it hardened. She lifted her hand in a wave and disappeared inside the house, the yellow door coming closed between them.

Hunter got in the car then, only to find Aunt Mabel had started talking with Westin about school. He listened to them talk for a few minutes, because she knew how to ask questions that got the boy talking, and Hunter had no idea how to do that.

He hadn't anticipated feeling awkward around his own son, but a tense ache rode in his shoulders.

"Mom says you have a dog," Westin said, turning toward him.

"I do," Hunter said. "Her name's Clara."

"She won't let me get a dog," he said. "Says I'm not home enough to take care of him."

"Oh, every boy should have a dog," Hunter said. "I'll take care of him while you're at school."

"Really?"

"Sure, he can live at my house." Hunter ignored the look Aunt Mabel tried to give him in the rear-view mirror. "You can come stay at my house too. See him while you're there." With a start, he realized that he should have some custody over his son. He might even be able to get full custody, if he told the judge his ex-wife had never even told him about the child. And Alice worked; Hunter didn't. He could take care of Westin full-time.

Even as he thought it, he knew his thinking bordered on false. He could barely take care of himself. And he wasn't going to drag Westin or Alice through the courts. He didn't want to hurt Alice. Well, maybe a little bit. Fine, a lot. But he didn't want to injure Westin, and she was the boy's mother. Hurting her would hurt him.

"That'd be great," Westin said, but Hunter wasn't sure what he'd said in the first place.

"So tell me what you like to do," Hunter said. "Fishing? Painting?"

"Have you ever been out to the fishing hole by the bell tower?" Westin asked, his face lighting up.

"Have I ever?" Hunter laughed and shook his head, glad the anxiety had left him. "I used to ride my bike up there every weekend."

"Mom won't let me ride my bike," Westin said, some of his earlier joy dissolving. "She says it's too far."

"Is it?" Hunter asked. He supposed times were different now, and he added, "I'll take you then. Once it warms up a bit, those fish will be ours."

"Yeah!" Westin cheered, and a new measure of happiness Hunter thought he'd never feel again soared through him.

Now, if he could figure out how to get rid of the poisonous thoughts about Alice, Hunter thought he might have a shot at a real life here in Hawthorne Harbor.

4

Alice pressed her back into the door, commanding herself not to open it again. Not to run to the window and watch the car roll out of her driveway. She'd been dropping Westin off at her mom's for years. Then school. He went to birthday parties and out to lunch with his grandfather. He knew how to survive without her. And heaven help Hunter if he got the boy talking, because sometimes Westin never stopped.

A smile touched her lips, quickly replaced by a sob. She'd cried most of the night, and she deserved the agony wrecking her insides.

She really should've told Hunter about his son. So many things might have been different if she had.

"You can't change the past," she muttered to herself as she marched down the hall to shower. She hadn't told him originally about the pregnancy, because up until the minute Westin was born, Alice hadn't known if she was going to keep the baby or not. She hadn't found out the gender. She'd basically gone on as if she didn't have a human life growing inside her.

Of course, that wasn't entirely true—she'd left Hawthorne Harbor for the duration of the pregnancy, as well as the first year afterward. That way, if anyone asked who the father was, she could claim to have met someone in British Colombia, where her aunt lived.

So her life had changed drastically once she'd seen those two little pink lines. But she wasn't sure until she delivered the baby boy if she'd keep him or not. She almost hadn't let the nurses bring him into her, but then she'd wanted to see his face.

It was love at first sight, and when he opened those eyes—so light and blue and gray and just like Hunter's... Alice had decided then to keep him, and name him Westin.

She'd returned to Hawthorne Harbor when Westin was a year old, and she'd finished nursing school a few years later. Her career at the hospital was in its fifth year, and while she thought of Hunter every day, the possibility of ever seeing him again had grown cold and distant.

Until yesterday.

Yesterday, her whole world had been turned upside down again, by the same man.

Alice got out of the shower, completely unsure if she'd

even washed her hair. The room smelled like strawberries, so she probably had. Back in the kitchen, she poured herself a cup of coffee and sipped it, wondering when Hunter would return with Westin. Wondering what to do with herself.

She hadn't had free time in eight years, and she honestly didn't know how to spend it. Alice had a few friends—the nurses from work, and a few other single moms, though a couple of them had found their happily-ever-after in the last couple of years. Janey and Gretchen still came to lunch if they could, but they'd moved on with new husbands and new babies.

At twenty-nine—soon to be thirty—Alice still had time to have more children. But she hadn't dated anyone since Westin's birth. Since Hunter. In her really quiet, really honest moments, she knew why.

She was still in love with him.

What would he say if she ever dared admit that out loud? Not that she ever would. The man looked at her with hooked daggers in his eyes. "And he has every right to," she said to her coffee cup. "So, what should I do today?"

She used to talk out loud to Westin as a baby, and they'd had an aged, rescue dog for a couple of years that pretended to listen to Alice when she asked herself questions. She loved to go to lunch with friends, and hold newborn babies, and walk on the beach. But the sky outside looked ready to dump buckets on the small beach town of Hawthorne Harbor, and Alice avoided getting soaked to the bone in January.

After opening the fridge, she pulled out the leftover chicken her mother had brought her from the deli. She had the staples needed to make chicken noodle soup, with the pasta from scratch, and cooking often released some of the worries and cares stored in her brain.

While measuring flour and salt, kneading in eggs, and rolling out the pasta down for the noodles, she riddled through why Hunter being back in town was troubling her. Of course, having the Magleby's as enemies was a bad idea. Mabel ran almost everything in town through her choice of donations, and the older woman was well-respected and cared for. Alice herself had just made bread for the woman a couple of months ago when it had been made known that Mabel had come down with a cold.

Hunter's parents had left town shortly after she had, and they didn't know about their grandson either. Another knife entered her chest. Her secrecy had affected so many more people than she'd imagined.

"Can I say I was young and stupid?" she asked the carrots on her cutting board. "Clueless and scared?" Because she had been all of those things. Her parents had already been furious about the wedding, and she hadn't even told them she was going to Aunt Patty's. Her father's sister had finally called them when Alice refused to leave and told her aunt the reason why.

She'd only been nineteen years old. Would she have to pay for her mistakes and foolish decisions forever?

"Possibly," she muttered as she laid a celery stalk on the board. Thankfully, she was skilled enough in the kitchen to think, talk to herself, and dice vegetables at the same time. Her father had lectured her about responsibility once Westin had been born, and yes, he'd said, *You might have to pay for youthful decisions for a long time.*

Her mother had encouraged her to write to Hunter and tell him about his son. Send pictures on the boy's birthday. Alice hadn't had the heart or courage to confess to her mother that while she'd taken the pictures and written the emails, she'd never sent them.

An idea bloomed to life inside her mind. She quickly wiped her hands on her apron and reached for her phone. She had thousands of pictures of her son on this device. She could send one to Hunter right now.

She touched the scroll bar on the right side and dragged it down, down, down to the last picture in the list. It was really the first picture, and it was Westin on the day he was born. Her heart beat like hummingbird wings in her chest, and she hesitated. Would he like to see this? Or would it only enrage him, remind him of what she'd robbed him of?

She'd known Hunter before, but he had changed so much since the last time she'd seen him. Physically and emotionally. He was wiser, stronger, bigger than the man she'd shared two wonderful days with on Victoria Island.

Hurrying now, before she lost her conviction, she tapped to share, and tapped his name in her contacts. Another tap, and the picture flew through the textosphere to Hunter's phone. He could do with it what he wanted.

This is the day Westin was born, she typed out quickly. March 29.

She had a whole birthing story, but she'd only shared that with her mom friends, and besides Hunter probably didn't need all the details. He didn't respond to her text either, and Alice continued putting together the chicken noodle soup.

The simple actions of stirring and measuring helped to calm her, and by the time the soup was finished, she felt more like herself than she had since running into Hunter at the hospital yesterday.

When two hours had passed and Hunter had neither returned with Westin nor responded to her text, Alice wondered if she should've committed to doing something besides hiding in the house and cooking. Perhaps she should've gone to see a movie. Or get her nails done. Luxuries she could afford on her nursing salary but which she hardly ever did, due to her long hours at the hospital and her motherly instinct to be home with her son.

Her phone chimed, and she practically pulled a muscle in her back as she lunged for it.

We're going swimming, Hunter had sent.

"Swimming?" Alice wondered aloud. Where would they do that in the middle of winter? And Westin hadn't taken his swimming trunks with him. It also annoyed her that Hunter hadn't asked her if it was okay if he took Westin swimming.

"He shouldn't have to ask," she told herself, still staring at the words. "He's his son too." And Westin knew how to swim. Loved swimming, actually, which was probably why Hunter wanted to take him. They were obviously getting along, and finding things to talk about, and Alice should be grateful.

But Hunter had just been reintroduced into their lives yesterday. How did he know that Alice didn't have something planned for that day? Maybe Westin had a big school project due on Monday or a friend's playdate arranged. Why did he assume he could take Westin for the entire day?

A sense of injustice wormed its way through her, no matter how hard Alice tried to push against it. But it wasn't fair. In that moment, she realized that while yes, she'd been worried about Hunter's reaction to finding out he had a son, she was also scared that Westin would like him more than he liked her.

She was jealous of Hunter.

"Maybe Doctor Lucas has an appointment today," she said to her phone as the screen darkened. Everything tangled inside her, and even her therapist wouldn't be able to undo this knot.

But she had to try, so she made the call.

Three hours later, her soup had simmered to perfection, and she'd had a good session with Dr. Lucas. Acknowledging how she felt was one of the hardest things for Alice, and she'd identified several emotions plaguing her.

Now, whether or not she could follow through on some of Doctor Lucas's suggestions...well, that would be the tricky part. Up first was talking to Hunter when he returned with Westin, which should be any moment now as he'd texted that they were on their way back from the new indoor pool that had just been built in nearby Bell Hill. That drive could only be about twenty-five minutes, and Alice had been sitting on the porch for forty now.

With her hands tucked deeply in the pockets of her hoodie, she watched the wind blow against the spindly, leafless branches. Winter held a special kind of beauty Alice rarely took the time to enjoy. In fact, she'd been so busy with school, then work, and always Westin, that Alice didn't often take time to enjoy much of anything.

When she had a few spare moments, she slept or watched TV for a while. Then she felt guilty and vowed to do better. Do better at what, she wasn't sure.

The sound of a car coming toward her drew her attention to the road. The shiny black car Hunter had arrived in that morning turned into her driveway, and she stood from the white wicker chair she'd been sitting in.

She recognized Jaime Allcott behind the steering wheel. He worked at the Mansion, and for Mabel apparently. He looked down at something on his phone while Mabel twisted around to the people in the back seat.

Finally, the back door opened, and Hunter got out. He moved with extreme care, the slowness of his motion extremely noticeable. She hoped the day with Westin hadn't injured him further, and true concern filled her.

Westin burst from the car behind him and ran up the sidewalk. "Mom! Look what I got at the aquatics center!" A huge, plastic blow-up dragon bounced against his side, and his face held pure delight.

"That's great," she said, wishing she'd been invited to go swimming with them. Dr. Lucas had said to be patient. Give Hunter the room and time he needed to bond with his son.

"You've had eight years to do that," she'd said. "And mothers always have a deep bond with their children, because they shared their bodies with them for nine months."

Be patient.

Give Hunter space and time.

She could do that. She could. Westin hugged her and ran with his dragon into the house. Alice probably would've turned and followed him, another half-hearted wave to the man she'd once loved enough to defy her parents and marry him.

But he came steadily toward her, using that cane she'd

seen him with in the hospital. He paused at the bottom of the steps, and she went down them to meet him. "How much for breakfast and lunch and swimming?" she asked. "Oh, and the dragon."

Hunter blinked at her. "I don't need your money."

Of course he didn't. He was Magleby royalty, chauffeured all over the county by his great aunt's driver.

"Did you—?" she started.

"Thank you for letting me have him for so long today." Hunter glanced up the steps, seemingly oblivious to the question she'd been about to ask. He looked at her again, his eyes so beautiful in this half-sunshine. "I would like to set up a meeting to discuss custody."

Custody.

The word ripped through her, stealing her breath. He was going to take Westin from her, and adrenaline made her heartbeat spike.

"I'm not going to take you to court, Alice," he said softly but firmly. She honestly preferred the indignant anger to this kindness. "But he's my son, and I want to spend time with him. I shouldn't have to ask you or arrange everything through you."

She pressed her lips together, the world spinning so, so fast. She hadn't even considered that Hunter would want custody of Westin. It made sense now that he'd said it, but she was still trying to catch up.

She studied the landscaping, trying to find something to seize onto that made sense. Custody. He wanted Westin to live with him sometimes. Pick him up from school and—

"So you and me," he said, jolting her back to the conversation. "You could come to my house, or I'll come here while he's at school. Lauren said she'd love to have Westin over to play with Porter one afternoon while we talk." He put his hand gently on the side of Alice's face and made her look at him. "But we need to meet—without him—and work out a custody agreement we can both live with."

Every instinct in her told her to lean into this man's touch and take all the comfort she could from it. His hand was warm and wonderful against her skin, but he dropped it quickly as they continued to gaze at one another.

"I'm off tomorrow," she said.

"So is he," Hunter responded. "Lauren's in Seattle until tomorrow night."

"My parents will take him," she said.

"Do you want to go to dinner?"

It took Alice a moment to realize he wasn't asking her out. They needed to meet to talk about custody, not to share their lives with each other. Hunter hadn't acted nor said anything that would indicate he was even remotely interested in her.

He just wanted to get the job done. Get an arrangement made so he didn't have to talk to her anymore. Deal with her again, just to see his son.

Her stomach flipped, sending a sickening pain down

both of her legs. "Dinner would be fine," she said. "Oh. I made you some soup." She dashed up the steps against a protest she barely heard and grabbed the bag from the table beside the wicker chair where she'd been sitting.

"Chicken noodle." She descended the steps again, taking them quickly back to Hunter's side. "And some left-over rolls I had. I know you just got back into town and all that." She held out the plastic bag with two quart-sized jars of soup and a half a bag of rolls she'd opened for breakfast sandwiches a couple of days ago.

When he didn't take it immediately, her heart fell to her feet. "Hunter—"

"Thank you," he said, finally taking the bag. "Let's meet at Swan's at six tomorrow." With that, he walked back to the car in slow, stuttered steps, the heavy bag of food swinging strangely from his left hand as he used the cane in his right.

She watched until he sank into the car and pulled the door closed behind him. Then she turned and went up the steps and into her house, refusing to look back. Number one, she didn't want him to know she still longed for him. And number two, he'd just barked the time and place of their meeting without asking her for her opinion.

That had always annoyed her, and while Hunter was charming, and gorgeous, and a war veteran, he still wasn't perfect.

5

Hunter slept for fifteen hours before he even stirred, and that was only to go to the bathroom and swallow more painkillers. He let Clara out while he leaned against the doorframe and waited for her to take care of her business, the rain a steady drizzle.

Then he quite literally stumbled back to bed—he was so tired of shuffling and limping everywhere he went— and fell back asleep. When he woke again, his body felt rusty, like he needed a wizard with an oil can to help him get out of bed and into the shower.

He was only thirty-one-years-old. He shouldn't feel this way for another few decades, and a flash of irritation mixed with injustice. Why had he had to be injured while in the line of duty?

Stop it, he told himself as he stepped into the hot spray.

It would loosen him up, and he'd eat, and everything would be fine.

He'd promised Aunt Mabel he'd come up for brunch this morning, and he was already dangerously close to being late. Everything took so long with his injuries, and he'd barely stepped out of the shower when his phone bleeped out a notification.

Jaime is on his way to get you, Aunt Mabel had texted. And Hunter was nowhere near ready to be picked up. He hurried as best as he could, but Jaime still sat in the living room with Clara for fifteen minutes before Hunter was ready to leave the house.

"I'm sorry," he said to the other man. "I overslept."

"Yesterday was a busy day." Jaime gave him a warm smile. "Is Clara coming?"

"Yes," Hunter said, deciding on the spot. "Come on, Clara. Let's go load up."

If possible, her doggy face lit up and she led the way toward the door. She didn't open it, as Jaime beat her to it and Hunter hadn't commanded her to. She stayed right by his side as he leaned on Jaime to get down the steps to the ground, and he went around to the passenger side front seat this time.

He exhaled as he sat in the seat, a sweat already worked up on his brow. "Thanks, Jaime," he said, unsure of whether or not he needed to clarify what his gratitude was for.

"Happy to do it, Hunter." He started the car and

started down the lane toward the main road. Hunter's house didn't sit that far away, but it sure felt secluded where he was. And in the spring and summer, when the trees would be in full bloom, he wouldn't even be able to see this road.

Jaime gave him the dignity of letting him walk by himself toward Aunt Mabel's cottage, while he went back up to the Mansion. Hunter knocked, surprised in the next moment to hear deep, male voices from within, one of which called, "Come in!"

Hunter turned the knob and said, "Go on, Clara," to his dog, who walked in a bit uncertainly. Then she darted forward, two other dogs already in the house. With two other men, both of whom were quite a bit older than Hunter. He recognized them both, though. It wasn't hard to stand out when one was the Chief of Police.

"Hey," he said, trying to find the man's name.

"You remember Adam Herrin," Aunt Mabel said from her spot on the couch. "And his brother Drew. He lives out at the Loveland Lavender Farm now."

"Of course," Hunter said, moving forward to shake their hands. "What are you guys doing here?"

"Oh, Mabel needed some oils," Drew said. "My wife sent me with some stuff."

"I came for the food," Adam said, holding up a cheese Danish. At least he was honest, and Hunter chuckled. "I'm headed into the station," he said. "Is that one of Trent's dogs?" He nodded toward Clara.

"Yep," Hunter said. "He and Lauren gave her to me when I got in on Thursday."

"He was a good cop," Adam said. "I'm happy for him, I am. I just miss him around the station sometimes." He looked at Drew. "Are you ready to go? Gretchen will be satisfied?"

"I think so," Drew said, glancing around. "We gave her the oils, the casserole, and the apron."

"I'm fine," Aunt Mabel said in her barking voice. "You boys go on. Hunter's here, and we need to chat."

"Oh, boy." Drew laughed, and Hunter wondered what it would be like to be that instantaneously happy. He'd been like that yesterday, with Westin, he supposed, and he smiled too.

"Good luck," Adam added as the brothers went out the front door. Westin moved over to the armchair and sat down.

"We need to talk?" he asked.

"Oh, heavens no. I was just saying that to get them to go." Aunt Mabel waved her wrinkled hand and said, "Are you hungry?"

"Starving," Hunter said, but he made no move to get up. "I slept forever, Aunt Mabel. Sorry I'm late."

"It's no bother." She got up and gathered a plate before loading it with baked goods. "Here you go."

He took the plate with what he hoped was a grateful grin and picked up an apple turnover. "When do you have time to make these?"

"I'm old," she said. "I'll sleep when I die."

He chuckled and shook his head. The apple turnover was ooey gooey flaky deliciousness, and Hunter enjoyed every bite. Aunt Mabel let him eat through a few pastries before she said, "What are you going to do about Alice?"

"Alice?" Hunter repeated. "I'm not going to do anything about Alice. There's nothing *to* do about Alice. It's Westin I need to do something about." He peered at her, because he hadn't been alone with her since he'd asked her if she'd known Westin was Hunter's son.

"When did you know he was mine?"

"Who?"

"Okay, I'm going home." Hunter braced his hands against the armrests, and he wasn't sure he could push himself up. He should probably reschedule with Alice, too. He managed to get himself standing, and he looked down at Aunt Mabel. "Thank you for letting me live in the cabin at the bottom of the hill," he said with genuine gratitude. "I really appreciate it."

Aunt Mabel stood too, and it was difficult for her as well. "You don't need to go, Hunter."

"I want to know the truth about Westin." His fingers instinctively curled into fists. "I *deserve* to know about my own son." As quickly as his irritation flared, it faded away. He exhaled and reached down to pat Clara. "I'm sorry, Aunt Mabel."

He was so tired of apologizing, but he managed a

weary smile in the general direction of his great aunt. "Thank you for the pastries."

"You're welcome."

He took a few steps toward the front door. "So you do respond to things."

"What?"

"I said thank you for the house, and you didn't respond. I asked you about Westin a couple of nights ago, and you never answered that either."

"That house was empty. Of course you can have it."

"Well, I want you to know I appreciate it." He glared at her.

"Fine, you're welcome." She huffed and folded her arms. "And I knew that little boy was yours the moment Alice came back to town with him."

Hunter retraced his steps and sat back down. "Came *back* to town with him?"

"She left Hawthorne Harbor about a month after you did. Came back two years later with that cute little boy— with Magleby eyes. Well, at least over on that Quinn side." She quirked up her lips. "They have that unique blue-gray, you know?"

"Yeah, I know." Hunter ran his hands through his hair. "Why didn't you tell me? You wrote me plenty of times."

"Wasn't my news to tell."

"Did anyone ever ask her about him?" Hunter wanted to ask dozens of other questions, and he wished Alice was in the room to answer them.

"I don't know, Hunter." She reached over and patted his hand. "You were such a good boy, and now you're an excellent man. You really should do something about Alice."

"Westin," Hunter said again.

"There's nothing to be done about him," Aunt Mabel said. "He's yours, and he loves you already. You love him. But what you need to figure out is if you love Alice."

Hunter scoffed, the idea so laughable, he actually laughed. When Aunt Mabel didn't join in, or even smile, he sobered. "What? You actually think...? Well, what do you think?"

"Oh, I'm old," Aunt Mabel said. "My mind barely works these days." She stood up again and patted his arm. "Stay as long as you want, but I have to get up to the Mansion." She started for the door. "I have a bride and her mother coming to look at menus."

"You walk up that hill yourself?" he asked, wishing he could jump to her aid. Her words rotated around and around in his head. *You need to figure out if you love Alice.*

"Yes," she said, picking up an intricately carved walking stick positioned by the door. "It's doable on good days, and today is a very good day." She smiled at him. "Let me know if you need Jaime to drive you anywhere. He's busy up here, but Westin is important."

"Thanks," Hunter said, and Aunt Mabel left. Her house felt so homey to him that Hunter stayed in the armchair, thinking.

He was hoping to get Alice to agree to bring Westin to his house and come pick him up. That didn't solve the times he'd want to take the boy to the movies or to the beach, but Hunter would tackle those problems one at a time. Lauren and Trent had a son near the same age, and perhaps Westin and Porter would get along great. Maybe Hunter wouldn't have to drive all over the place to entertain his son.

And he did not have feelings for Alice, other than frustration and fury. Did he? Sure, his heart pumped harder at the sight of her, but that was because of what she'd done. Not because she was still the most beautiful creature he'd ever seen, or that she was the only woman he'd ever loved.

Loved. Past tense.

Right?

Clara lifted her head and looked at the front door, and a moment later, someone knocked. He looked at the door and back to his dog. "Answer it," he said, wondering if she could open any door or just the one at his house.

Clara trotted over to the door and jumped up, using her nose to open the door just the way she did at home. The door drifted open a few inches, and she pawed at it to get it to go farther.

"Oh, hello," an older man said, poking his head inside. "Mabel?"

Hunter lifted his hand, his curiosity off the charts. "Hey," he said. "Aunt Mabel went up to the Mansion."

"Hunter?"

He squinted at the man, trying to place him in his memory. He couldn't. "I'm sorry, I don't know you."

"Clyde Brower. I was your grandfather's best friend." He strode across the room—well, as fast as a man his age could stride—and shook Hunter's hand. "Where's your dad these days?"

"Oh, he and my mom moved down to Southern California. Wanted a warmer beach." He smiled and waited for Clyde to explain why he was there. He did remember the guy from a couple of family parties. When he didn't say anything else, Hunter asked, "Are you still doing magic?"

Clyde laughed, the sound loud and booming. "No. Not even a little bit." He glanced around. "Well, Mabel had something for me. Do you think she left it out?"

"She didn't say anything."

"I'll go ask her." Clyde nodded, smiled, and left. Hunter decided he should go too, and he took his time getting to his feet and out the door. The world before him felt huge and wonderful. Down the hill, he could just make out the roof of Lauren's house, and his eyes traveled down the road to the left to his own.

Clara sat at his side, surveying the town of Hawthorne Harbor, situated more to his right. "It's pretty, right?" he asked the dog. Not surprisingly, the canine didn't answer. Hunter started up the path toward the Mansion, thinking that if his eighty-something-year-old great aunt could climb this hill, so could he.

On a good day, he thought as he took step after step. His foot slipped, and he tried to compensate with his injured leg. That didn't work, and Hunter knew he was going down before his knee hit the dirt path.

He grunted in pain and rolled onto his back, sliding down the path only a few feet. His heart pounded, and he sucked at the air. "I'm fine," he told himself.

Clara whined and licked his face. "I'm fine," he told her, wishing he could command his heart to settle down as well. He blinked, and he saw dense forest above him when he opened his eyes again. The sound of gunfire surrounded him. The scent of smoke and burnt flesh. He rolled onto his side, but that sent shooting, burning pain from his hip to his knee to his ankle, where everything tingled and dulled into nothing.

Clara licked him again, bringing him back to this moment. This moment, here, in Hawthorne Harbor. He wasn't on the ship. Wasn't in life-threatening danger.

He also wasn't getting up by himself.

"Clara," he said to the dog. "Clara, go get Jaime. You remember Jaime from this morning? Go get Jaime. Go."

The dog trotted away, up toward the Mansion, then whined and turned back to him. "Go," he commanded in his military voice. "Get Jaime. Get someone." He laid his head on the hard ground, hoping the last thing he heard wasn't the clicking of dog claws against hard-packed dirt.

6

"You're going to stay with grandma tonight, Westie," Alice said to her son. "Get your backpack, and make sure you have clean clothes and unders for school tomorrow." She pushed her hand through her hair and sighed as she looked around her son's room. It was littered with building blocks, toys, a skateboard, his abandoned baseball equipment, and his dirty clothes.

"And you're going to have to clean this room tomorrow after school."

"I have piano tomorrow after school," he said, getting down on the floor to pull his backpack out from under his bed. He unzipped it, and a foul smell nearly punched Alice in the chest.

"What is that?" she asked.

"I forgot I had a ham sandwich in there," he said,

taking out a bag that contained the remains of the sandwich.

Alice made a face and left the room in favor of grabbing the garbage can out of the bathroom next door. "Put that here," she said upon returning to Westin's room. He dropped it in, and her annoyance at the uncleanliness of his room almost had her barking at him to start cleaning it up right now.

But she was already late in leaving to drop him off at her mother's and get over to Swan's at the appointed meeting time. Knowing Hunter, he was probably already there. Sitting up straight and drinking only water. A smile touched her lips when she remembered he didn't like the sting of carbonation in his throat.

And she loved it. Drank eighty ounces of diet cola on every shift just to make it through.

"Ready," Westin announced, and Alice realized she was still holding the garbage can. She took it with her into the kitchen and set it beside the bigger one that needed to be emptied there.

Dropping Westin at her parents' went smoothly, because he did it several times a week. He slept there a lot, but she'd been on a week of day shifts, then had this glorious weekend off before starting back on the nightshift.

She preferred nights, as they were slower, and she didn't have to leave Westin with her parents. She felt like a zombie a lot of the time, but even zombies could be good moms. If she was there, she did fine. If she had to be at work, she couldn't be a mom. So she'd rather be a zombie mom than not one at all.

Drawing a deep breath, she realized that Hunter was going to be taking Westin from her. Whether that was rational or not, it was true. He wanted custody, he wanted to have Westin at his house, he wanted to be the boy's father.

"Those are all good things," she told herself. At the same time, it hurt to think that Westin wouldn't need her as much.

She got herself into the restaurant by an act of God, and she said, "I'm meeting someone here. Hunter Magleby?"

"Oh, are you Alice Kopp?" The young woman looked down and pulled a slip of paper out by the corner. "He called about ten minutes ago. Said he's not going to make it."

Alice's eyes widened, and she flinched away from the woman. "Not going to make it?" She'd been starving herself since breakfast so she'd be nice and hungry for this meal. Then she'd eat, and he wouldn't think she was too nervous around him. Her stomach was about to wage war on every other organ in her body, because now she was starving on top of panicked.

"That's what he said. I wrote it down." She handed Alice the slip of paper and grabbed a handful of menus. "Raven, six."

Alice moved out of the way as the larger group went past her and followed the girl between tables. The note was hastily written. It had her name and Hunter's name on it. Then "not going to make it."

No other explanation.

Alice looked out the window at the darkness that had already blanketed the world. It was barely six o'clock, but it felt like midnight, and she wondered why she hadn't taken Westin and moved somewhere warmer. Somewhere thousands of miles from here. Then Hunter would've never found out about his son, and she wouldn't be dealing with any of this right now.

She banished the thoughts, because she'd already made some bad decisions in her life. She couldn't heap on selfishness too.

"Well," she said to her reflection in the glass. "If he can't come here, I'll go to him." After all, the man couldn't drive. So he'd have to be home. Right?

Alice didn't like the idea of Hunter living out on Forgotten Road, but she'd already been there once, and she'd probably have to go a lot more once she worked out a custody agreement with him. She knew his cousin Lauren lived nearby, as Trent Baker had listed his house for sale last year, and Alice had wanted to buy it with every fiber of her being. The back yard was exquisite, with a custom-built deck that could've been a sanctuary all its own.

But she didn't have enough money, and she'd stayed in

the little two-bedroom house that was closer to her parents.

The drive seemed to take no time at all, and she wondered why Hunter hadn't just called or texted her when he knew he couldn't make it. There was something wrong. Oh, yes, Alice's radar was firing, and not on good cylinders.

She found the right road, easing down off the main highway that led up to the Mansion, and saw Hunter's house ablaze with lights. So someone was home. Two cars were parked out front, which sent up red flags to go with the blasting radar. Was he having a party? He cancelled their custody meeting for that?

She almost turned around and went home. No custody meeting meant she could keep things how they were for a little longer.

But something told her there wasn't a party going on inside Hunter's house. The man liked to have a good time, sure. "You mean the younger man you once knew," she muttered to herself as she pulled in beside the last car.

The truth was, she didn't know Hunter at all anymore. But she felt like she knew enough to know he hadn't joined the Marines and then turned into a party animal.

Sure enough, she heard no music as she approached the front door. She raised her hand to knock, regretting so many of her life choices in that single moment. Her fist against the wood sounded like a threat, and she stopped after only three times.

Someone—not a dog—opened the door, and she found Trent Baker himself standing there. "Alice?" he asked.

She knew him; he knew her. It was a small town, and his son had been brought into the ER a couple of years ago while she worked the night shift there. "Good evening," she said. "Is Hunter home?"

"Well, yeah, but—" Trent backed up and fell silent when Lauren joined him.

"He called the restaurant," she said without a smile. "He can't meet tonight, unfortunately."

"Why not?" Alice asked, the scent of cleaning supplies mixed with something savory meeting her nose. "Is he all right?"

"I'm afraid not," Lauren said. "He fell this morning, and—"

"He fell?" Alice took a step forward as if she'd enter the house, concern crashing through her. "Did you take him to the hospital?"

"He went to a physical therapy session," Lauren said, moving to stand shoulder-to-shoulder with Trent so Alice couldn't get by. "He's really tired and in a lot of pain right now."

Alice clutched her purse, unsure of what to do. "I'm a nurse."

"He'll be okay," Lauren said at the same time Hunter called from inside, "It's fine, Lauren. She can come in if she wants to." His voice sounded weak, raspy, like he'd just gotten up.

Lauren looked at Trent and then over her shoulder, indecision raging in her expression.

"We need to get Porter home," Trent said in a low voice. "Maybe she can sit with him for an hour or two."

Sit with him? He needed a babysitter? Alice wanted to volunteer, say she'd sat with many patients over the years, which of course, she had. But she didn't want to seem overeager to stay, and she didn't want Hunter to hear her call him a patient.

So, she stood there, mute and waiting for Lauren's decision. She finally sighed and backed up a step. "All right. Come in." She looked at Trent. "Go get Porter, and let's go now." She tossed a disgruntled look at Alice and crossed over to Hunter. "We have to get Porter home, okay? And Trent has to take care of the dogs. I'll be back in an hour. Alice is here, and she's going to sit with you."

Only a single lamp lit the room, but it was still plenty bright enough to see the heated edge of Hunter's gaze. "Fine," he said, his lips barely moving.

Trent came down the hall with Porter, and they gathered up their bags and dogs and left. Alice took a few steps closer and perched on the edge of the recliner.

"Why couldn't you call me?" she asked.

"My phone was a casualty of the fall." He wouldn't look at her, and she wondered if he was embarrassed or angry. Probably both. "I used Lauren's to call the restaurant." He flicked his eyes in her direction. "You don't need to stay. I'm fine."

"Lauren said—"

"Lauren worries a little too much," Hunter interrupted.

Alice hated being cut off, but she pressed her lips together and focused on the floral design of her purse. Maybe then it wouldn't hurt so much that he couldn't even look at her. "You fell?"

"I don't want to talk about it."

A boldness filled her she didn't know she had. She'd dealt with difficult patients before, and that was all he was. A difficult patient. "Well, Hunter," she said. "We need to talk about it, if I'm going to let my son come spend time here with you."

"He's *my* son too," Hunter shot back. "And I have every right to see him."

She lifted her eyes to his, and they glared at one another.

"I do not want to take you to court to see him," he said. "But I will if I have to. He's *my* son, and you've already taken eight years from me." His chest heaved, and he groaned, but he did not look away from her. "Eight years, Alice."

She wanted to ask him how much of it he would've missed anyway, but she didn't. It wasn't fair, and it would only be something she'd regret later. She drew a deep, calming breath that actually did little to pacify the nervous energy tapdancing through her. "Right now, my parents take him on nights I have to work. I'm in four or five nights a week, usually twelve-hour shifts. He goes there just after dinner, sleeps there, and they take him to school in the morning. I pick him up afterward, and we spend the afternoon together."

"I can do all of that," he said. "I want to get to know him. He's a great kid."

"Thank you," Alice said, as if she'd done everything with him herself. "He seemed to really like you too."

Hunter's face lit up like a Christmas tree. "Yeah?"

Alice giggled and nodded. "Yes, Hunter. He likes you." She stood up and moved into the kitchen. "Do you have two bedrooms here?"

"Yes, and one bath. It's small, but it's okay. I'll get him everything he needs."

Alice didn't need to go down the hall and check. Knowing Mabel Magleby, this place had been cleaned weekly, even when no one lived here. "I'll keep you apprised of my schedule. It does change sometimes. I usually do a rotation of day shifts every few months."

"And you prefer graveyards?"

Alice had not been prepared for the conversation to turn toward her. She looked at Hunter as she moved back around the couch and into the living area. "Yes," she said. "Then I actually see Westin. If I work days, the only time I see him is when he sleeps."

Hunter nodded. "You're a good mom, Alice."

"I try," she said simply, trying to hold onto the tonalities in his voice when he'd said her name. Before, she'd loved hearing him whisper her name right before he kissed her. The sound was filled with love and backed up by the action to prove it.

"I want to be a good dad, too."

"You will be," she said.

"I fell trying to walk up the path from my great aunt's house to the Mansion. So it wasn't around here or because I was doing something normal."

"Why would you do that?" she asked.

His jaw tightened as he ground his teeth together, and he looked away. "I didn't have a ride home."

Her heart tore, and Alice simply looked at him. Could she blurt out that she still had feelings for him? What if they were one-sided, and he was as angry with her and as over her as he seemed to be? What if the only reason they were having this conversation was because of Westin? And without him, he'd have said hello in the hospital and gone on his way.

When their eyes finally met again, Alice decided she had to be brave. She had to say something. She had to be willing to risk her heart, something she hadn't been willing to do all those years ago.

"Hunter," she said slowly, still trying to find the right words. "Do you think...I mean, is there any chance of us... becoming a family again?"

He didn't miss a beat when he said, "We never were a family, Alice."

"Right, I know," she said, her throat so, so dry. "But do you think we could make one? Me, and you, and Westin?" She wished her voice didn't sound like she'd just inhaled helium, but the words were out.

He squirmed and reached over and stroked his dog. "I don't know, Alice."

"Is there even a tiny chance?" she asked, her heart thundering in her chest at what she was about to reveal. "Because I think we have a chance. I want a chance. But if you don't think we have one—even a tiny, little chance— I'll walk out the door and just bring Westin over at night. No more questions asked."

He sure took his sweet time answering, the way he had when they dated that glorious summer a decade ago. Her patience teetered, and she almost sighed and stormed out when he said, "I think there's probably a tiny chance. A really tiny chance. Like, so tiny it's microscopic."

Hope filled her, pushing her lips up into a smile and making her heart sing. "I'll take it."

7

Hunter felt like he'd been hit by a truck. It had taken about ten minutes for someone to find him on the path. Thankfully, it had been Jaime and Clara, with Mable and Clyde coming down after them.

Humiliation hit him again, something it had been doing on and off all day. He hated that he couldn't get up. Hated that he'd then been taken to the hospital, where they'd poked him and pushed him and made him do things that made his hip and knee throb no matter how much ice he put on it and how much painkiller he took.

Lauren had brought him dandelion root and turmeric, which was supposed to promote joint heath. He didn't have the heart to tell her he'd been blown up, and he didn't think dandelions could fix that.

Honestly, he wasn't sure anything could fix him. Having Clara against his good leg comforted him, but the numbness in his right foot still bothered him. The soft sound of Alice's breathing told him he wasn't alone, and that was nice too.

He'd been alone for so long, and it felt like he'd rejoined the human family. Alice hadn't said anything else since declaring she'd take the tiny, microscopic chance he'd given her that they could get back together and build a family with Westin.

Hunter had closed his eyes and evened his breathing, but he wasn't asleep. He'd been sleeping so much lately, but he was still tired. He wondered if this level of exhaustion would always accompany him, much like the tingling in his foot.

He hoped not. He wanted to do something more with his life. Before his father had left town, he'd had a successful lawn care business. Hunter had grown up mowing lawns and trimming hedges and moving gravel. He'd been good at it, and he liked the physical work.

He snorted softly at his thoughts. Had he really just thought he liked the physical work? He couldn't even walk up a path without falling. There was no way he could navigate uneven ground, or balance himself while carrying heavy things with his leg the way it was.

But he needed to do something. He'd gotten a great severance package from the Marines, and he had health-care for life. But he didn't want to stay cooped up in this cabin all day and all night.

And he wouldn't. He had Westin now, and the boy had

brought more hope and happiness into his life than he'd imagined a child could.

"Alice?" he asked, opening his eyes.

"Mm?" She looked up from her phone, and her dark eyes latched onto his. She really was a beautiful woman, and with more experience and more wisdom behind her, she possessed another kind of beauty he hadn't seen in her before.

"Why didn't you tell me about Westin?"

Fear entered those eyes, and she gave him a wobbly smile. She'd grinned at him like that when he'd asked her if she'd still go through with their wedding if her parents didn't come. They'd threatened to boycott it, and she'd flashed that shaky smile and said yes, she'd go through with it.

And she had. But it had seemed like she'd regretted that decision the moment he'd left town.

"That's the million dollar question, isn't it?" she asked.

"So you don't know?" he asked.

"There are a million little reasons," she said. "And I thought they were good at the time. And so I went through another day, or another month, or another year before something else or someone else would trigger my guilt. Then I'd find another excuse."

Hunter understood that, he really did. He had found any little reason he could not to return to Hawthorne Harbor. So it wasn't quite the same, but he could at least understand the power of rationalizing why he thought he'd been right.

"Name one of the excuses," he said.

"Well, for example, I wasn't even sure I wanted the baby, so I certainly didn't need to tell you I was pregnant. That got me through the first nine months."

Hunter cocked his head. "You were going to put the baby up for adoption?"

"I wasn't sure. I avoided making a decision. I wasn't even going to see him." She gave a half shrug, but her eyes were glassy with tears. "But then they handed him to me, and he was this perfect little bundle, and he smelled so good, and he opened his eyes." She shook her head, her tears splashing her cheeks.

She wiped at them quickly. "They were your eyes, and I was still so in love with you."

Hunter wanted to get up and kneel in front of her. Take both of her hands in his and beg her to tell him why she'd annulled their marriage if she loved him so much. But he couldn't get up, and his own emotions balled up in his throat.

"So I kept him, and I decided to make a life for us here. I went to school. I told myself I didn't need anyone's help—certainly not yours. I got a good job, and you never came back, and I told myself you didn't need to know. That you had a life—probably a wonderful, happy life— somewhere else. And I didn't say anything."

Hunter's life had not been wonderful or happy, but he didn't tell her that.

"And, this is one of the stupidest ones, but I didn't want him to the be the reason you came back to Hawthorne Harbor." She looked away and swiped at her eyes again. "I wanted you to come back when you were ready."

Hunter watched her, and there was more to what she'd said, but she kept it silent. "I'm not sure why it took me nine years," he admitted, clearing his throat afterward.

"Some things take a long time to decide upon," she said, reaching over the armrest and taking his hand in hers. Hunter squeezed her fingers, a measure of hope and forgiveness moving through him that was powerful and peaceful. He sighed and closed his eyes again, the warmth and weight of Alice's hand in his making him feel less lonely and more human, and he'd never expected to feel that in Hawthorne Harbor.

"I'm sure my mother will feel...she'll be upset if we take Westin away from her completely. And he does love his grandparents."

"I understand," Hunter said. "Maybe we could talk to Westin about it. I need time to get a room ready for him, and after that, I'd love to have him here in the evenings and take him to school."

"About that...." Alice said.

"I can't drive," he said, filling in the rest of her sentence. "So maybe that's the compromise. Maybe your mother could come here and take Westin to school." Just saying it out loud made him feel like a jerk. Her mother had never liked him. Was he really going to have to face the woman every morning and pass his son to her?

Yes, he thought. And he could change. She'd probably changed too. It had been ten years. Things changed.

"I'd get to see him, and she'd get to as well."

"I work most weekends," she said, but you could have him those days. Honestly, she'd probably like a break. She's no spring chicken anymore." Alice smiled as she said it, but Hunter knew his presence in Hawthorne Harbor affected a lot of lives. And here he'd thought he'd come back quietly, without pomp or circumstance, and find a way to fade into the fabric of small town life, the way he once had.

She didn't say anything else. Hunter didn't either. He just held her hand and listened to her breathe.

THE FOLLOWING DAY, HUNTER USED AN OLD PHONE OF Lauren's to call the furniture store and order a bedroom set for a little boy, one with a dresser and a bed and a nightstand and a lamp with dinosaurs on it. He didn't know his son that well, but he figured if Westin hated dinosaurs, they could get a new lampshade. Hunter had recently learned the wonders of online shopping, and he'd set up an account for grocery delivery and one for food delivery too—something called Restaurant Runner.

All he had to do was put in an order through them, and someone would go to the restaurant, pick it up, and deliver it to him. So he'd solved some of his driving issues, but he couldn't get Westin's third grade teacher to come pick him up in the morning.

Alice had left last night with the agreement that she'd bring Westin over to the cabin after school, and they'd all talk about the situation. Then she'd talk to her mother, and once everyone was in agreement and on-board, Hunter would start to have Westin in the evenings and overnight while Alice worked.

He'd had no idea what his life in Hawthorne Harbor would be like, but this wasn't it. His house sat on Forgotten Road, and he honestly thought he'd be forgotten. But as soon as he got off the phone with the furniture store, it rang again.

It was Lauren's old number, and he ignored the call. It ended and immediately started ringing again. He picked it up and said, "Hello?"

"Oh, you sound grouchy," a woman said. "It's Lauren. Can I bring you lunch? Or are you feeling up to getting out of the house?"

Hunter considered her questions. "You know what? I think I can get out for a bit."

"I'm working near the pier today. I'll come get you, and there are lots of choices in that part of town."

"Okay," Hunter said. "Can I bring Clara?"

"Of course. She loves riding in the back of my truck."

Several minutes later, Lauren pulled up to his house, and he was already waiting at the bottom of the steps. "Up," he said to Clara, and she jumped in the back of the truck, clearly enjoying the trip already. Hunter was glad he'd agreed to get out of the house—for Clara. She was a great dog, but she needed to run sometimes.

Hunter realized in that moment that both of his arms functioned just fine. He could throw a ball for his dog and have her retrieve it. She was a golden retriever, after all. "I'll get you a hot dog on the pier," he told his dog as he opened the passenger seat and put his left leg up on the truck's runner and balanced on his cane to get in the vehicle.

It was easier than last time, and he didn't mind the jostling quite so much either. They arrived at the pier a few minutes later, and she hopped out. Hunter followed much slower, and she said, "I'm headed over to the burger place."

"I promised Clara a hot dog," he said, looking at the boardwalk at the pier. He could walk on this. He'd just have to go slow. "Come on, Clara." The dog came over to his side and they set off down toward the hot dog stand at the end of the pier.

Hunter moved slowly, and while there was a decent amount of foot traffic during this lunch hour, no one seemed to mind. He whistled and watched the waves hit against the pier.

"Hunter?"

He turned around at the familiar voice and looked at the man that had been walking the other way. "Shaun Kim." A smile appeared on his face, and Hunter almost forgot he needed to find something to hold before he could shake his childhood friend's hand.

Shaun solved that problem for him anyway, because he grabbed onto Hunter, cane and all, and slapped him on the back. "I didn't know you were back in town," Shaun bellowed in his ear. "Why didn't you call me?"

"Well, I don't really have a phone right now." Hunter laughed and reached for the railing when Shaun let go of him. "Besides, I didn't know you were still in town."

"Oh, yeah. Never left. You're the one who lived all the adventures." Shaun grinned at him. "What are you doing these days?"

Hunter had no idea how to respond. "Getting things settled," he finally said as someone called Shaun's name.

He waved down the pier to them. "That's my crew. I manage a construction crew."

"Oh, that's great." At one point in his life, Hunter could've seen himself working construction. He loved the way something came together out of random pieces, and he liked the physical labor.

Sitting around was definitely going to kill him slowly.

He needed something to do during the day, a job without weekend work.

"Do all of your guys work on-site?" he asked Shaun.

"Not everyone," he said. "Why? You looking for something?"

"Yes," he said. "But." He lifted the cane. "I'm decent with a computer, and I led more than one team through tactical drills."

His men called him again, and he started walking backward without a thought for the uneven boardwalk. "I'll call you." He turned and walked away.

How he was going to call Hunter when he didn't have a phone—which was what Hunter had told him? Hunter wasn't stupid just because he was injured. Shaun wasn't going to give him a job.

He turned away from his friend's back and continued toward the hot dog stand, but his step wasn't nearly as vibrant as it had been before.

His phone buzzed, and the message was a picture of Westin when he was a baby. *First smile* sat under the picture, and the baby grinning back at him made his whole soul glow.

Alice had said nothing about the daily pictures she'd started to send him, and neither had he. But she'd sent three so far, and they'd become a lifeline for him...to her.

8

———

Alice spent her lunchtime in the middle of the night looking through old pictures and making notes of which photos to send to Hunter when. Nothing had been said between them about her image texts, but she knew he'd seen them.

She smiled at the pictures of Westin in the kitchen sink for bath time, and the video of the first steps he'd taken. She was going to get Hunter up to speed on all of Westin's best moments in the course of a month, even if she had to send him more than one picture per day.

When she realized she hadn't eaten yet, she wolfed down the sandwich she'd packed for herself and hurried back to the nurse's station.

"There you are," Sadie said.

"I'm not late," Alice said, setting her phone in the

cubby inside the office and turning back to her friend. "What's going on?"

"Doctor Bear," she muttered right before Dr. Scoville rounded the corner, his angular features already dark.

Surprise and dread darted through her at the same time. She wondered where Dr. Murphy had gone, as he'd been here before Alice's break. "Hello, Jeremy," she said, glancing at Sadie. The blonde ducked her head and studied something on a chart she didn't need to look at.

"Room 3523 needs clean sheets," he said, no greeting in sight. He handed Alice the chart. "And someone needs to call housekeeping to get those mop buckets out of the thirty hallway." He glanced around the counter. "Where'd my coffee go?"

So he'd been called in, and he wasn't happy about it. Alice didn't see a coffee cup anywhere, but she felt a great need to find it so the doctor she and the other nurses had nicknamed Bear would go back to his den until they needed him. On the night shift, they rarely needed a doctor as the patients usually slept peacefully through the night. They monitored pain and helped those get up and walk who needed to after surgeries. She sometimes rocked kids, or helped parents get ice chips for their children, or made sure the paperwork from the busy day when she wasn't there was ready for another hectic day in the children's wing.

"Maybe you finished it," Sadie said, sliding the chart she'd been reading into its slot.

"I didn't finish it."

Leah, another nurse, came around the corner. Alice glanced at her, and she said, "Looks like Leah's got it."

"It was in Alyssa's room." She handed Bear his drink, and the three nurses exchanged a glance.

"Thank you," he said, rounding the corner and stepping past Sadie to get to the office. He nudged the door almost all the way closed and sat at the desk. Ah, the bear was in his den, and the tension on the whole floor slipped down a notch.

Alice exhaled. "I'll take care of the pain meds."

"I'll call housekeeping," Sadie said, reaching for the phone.

Leah leaned over and said, "We should put them all in the office," she said with a mischievous grin. "Say that's where they told us to store them until they can come up."

Alice suppressed a giggle as she walked away. She smiled to herself as she logged the medication she took from the closet and went down the hall to Alyssa's room. The little girl was awake, the glow from a tablet playing across her face.

"You're hurting?" she asked the eight-year-old. She glanced at her mother, who looked worse than Alice had seen her before.

Alyssa nodded, her eyes wide and round. Alice smiled at her and said, "I'm going to get that taken care of. You'll be feeling better in no time." She injected the painkillers into the girl's IV. "And in the morning, we'll see how you're doing, and maybe that IV can come out."

She beamed down at the girl, so much love flowing through her. After all, Westin could by lying in this bed after falling out of a tree. He could have the broken leg, and she could be the exhausted mother in the uncomfortable armchair beside the bed.

"Thank you," the mom said, and Alice smiled at her.

"Call me if you need anything," she said. "Try to get some sleep." She pulled the door closed behind her, making sure not to leave any personal items behind in the room the way Bear had done. Technically, she could report him, but she wouldn't. Neither would Sadie or Leah. They watched out for each other. They weren't supposed to use their phones while on shift, but sometimes the graveyard shift was so boring.

Back at the station, she sighed and sat down to go through a couple of charts she hadn't looked at before her lunch break. The patients were sleeping fine, but she still wanted to know who was on the floor during her shift.

"How are things with your soldier?" Sadie asked.

Alice's pulse pinged up to the back of her throat. How was that even possible? "He's...fine." She didn't need to get into all the details about custody and holding his hand in the dim light of his cabin. Her skin tingled just thinking about it.

"Fine?" Sadie asked. "Oh, that's got an interesting story written all over it."

"No," Alice said. "It was the most uninteresting weekend ever."

Sadie scoffed and laughed. "You have never been a good liar." She gathered her hair back into a ponytail. "Which means you saw him, and talked to him, and have something to say about him."

"He's Westin's father," Alice said. "I have to talk to him. He came to get Westin, so yes, I saw him." She would not gossip about him to her girlfriends, so the hand-holding stayed a secret.

"Oh, you still like him."

Alice sighed and gave up on the chart in front of her. She turned toward Sadie, trying to be annoyed but failing. "Yes, okay," she practically hissed. "I still like him. I've always liked him." She shook her head, her own dark hair brushing her forearms. "Sadie...."

"What?" Her friend sobered and searched Alice's face. She reached over and touched Alice's hand. "What?"

Alice tried to figure out what. She wasn't sure she could say it out loud. "I like him," she said, cocking her head and shrugging one shoulder. "And he said we have a tiny, microscopic chance of having something again. So...."

Sadie squealed. "So you're going to get back together with him."

"No," Alice said when she really wanted to say yes. "I mean, I don't know." She stared blankly at the folder in front of her. "I loved him, you know? Those feelings bubble up from time to time, especially because I see his face every time I look into Westin's."

Sadie squeezed her hand. "So maybe just see if you can love him again."

"I'm sure I can," she whispered. "The problem is, can he ever love me again?" She looked at Sadie, really looked at her. She saw the concern in her friend's eyes, and Alice drew in a deep breath.

"He's very angry with me, as he should be. It could be a very long road to forgiveness."

"Well," Sadie said. "Good thing you're very good at taking long roads." She lifted her eyebrows. "Right? I mean, who goes to nursing school with a toddler? That was really hard. Raising him yourself has been hard. You can do this hard thing too."

"I had help with all of that," she said, her voice a ghost of itself. "My mother helped me every step of the way." She shook her head, hot tears pricking her eyes yet again. "And I was alone for most of the day Saturday, and it was hard. And now Hunter wants custody of Westin, and I have to tell my mom that he gets to have Westin and not her. When she's helped for so long." Desperation and despair dove through her.

"It's the right thing," she continued. "I know it is. But it's going to be an adjustment."

"Have you talked to your mom yet?" Sadie asked.

Alice shook her head. "Not yet." She wasn't sure what she was waiting for. It had been four days since she'd talked with Hunter about dropping Westin off at his place after dinner and before bedtime. She knew Hunter had ordered furniture for their son, as he'd sent pictures of the room as it came together.

She just needed to talk to her mother. Why was talking to people so difficult for her?

"I just don't want her to feel bad," Alice said.

"She won't feel bad," Sadie said, squeezing her hand again. "She's your mom, and she loves you and Westin. I'm sure she wants you to be happy. And if Hunter makes you happy...." Sadie trailed off and shrugged. She lifted her soda to her lips and sucked. "Now, if you're okay with it, I'd like to talk about the cute man I met downstairs last night."

Alice's eyebrows went up. "You met a cute man downstairs last night?"

"As I was coming in. I think he's a new paramedic or something. He was wearing a uniform." She purred. "And wow, he was wearing it well." She giggled, and Alice couldn't help laughing too.

"So help me find out who he is," Sadie said. "You've worked in the ER loads of times. Maybe you need to go down there tonight or something."

Alice grinned at her. "You know what? I totally need to go down there tonight." She stood and grabbed her forty-four-ounce diet soda. "I'll be back in a few minutes."

ALICE GROANED WHEN HER ALARM WENT OFF, BUT SHE rolled over and silenced it before getting up. She had to talk to her mother today. Westin got out of school in an hour, and she'd promised Hunter he could have the boy for the afternoon and evening. He wanted to show Westin his bedroom and fix anything before Monday night came.

Monday night.

Only four days away. She had to talk to her mother this afternoon. She seized onto Sadie's words that her mother wouldn't feel bad. That she loved Alice and Westin and wanted them both to be happy.

But Alice knew her mother had never liked Hunter all that much, and Alice worried that she wouldn't want to give up the time with her grandson for him.

"Doesn't matter," Alice said. If she and Hunter had stayed married, her mom wouldn't have a choice. And if Hunter took Alice to court, none of them would have a choice. She showered and drove the few blocks her mother's house.

"Mom?" she called as she entered the house.

"In the kitchen." She came out with soapy suds on her hands. "What are you doing here? I wasn't expecting to see you today."

Alice had the night off, so Westin would be sleeping at home. "I know." Alice sighed. "Mom...." She looked into her mother's eyes, her courage almost failing. Her throat felt like sandpaper. She pushed past it and said, "Hunter would like partial custody of Westin."

Her mom blinked and then acceptance came across her face. "Of course he does." She turned and went back into the kitchen. "And he should have it."

"You'll still get to see Westin," Alice said, following her. "Just not as much. Hunter would...Hunter and I talked, and we agreed that it would be best if, on nights I'm working, Westin went to his place after dinner. Sometimes before dinner. And stayed there for the night. He'll get him ready for school."

"It's a good plan," her mother said, rinsing the last pan and placing it on the towel beside the sink. She dried her hands and turned toward Alice.

"We both still need your help," she said, swallowing. "Hunter can't drive Westin to school, so he's asking if you'd come to his place on Forgotten Road, pick up Westin, and take him to school. I'll pick him up as usual."

Her mother's eyes, so dark like her own, lit up. "Of course I can do that."

"It's only a few minutes, but—"

"I'm happy to help, even if it's only a few minutes."

"You're helping Hunter." Alice watched her mom, hoping to see some sign of acceptance from her.

Her mother's lips pressed into a thin line, but she smiled quickly after that. "I don't hate Hunter."

"You've certainly never liked him."

She sighed. "This isn't about how I feel about Hunter," she said. "No, I didn't like him when you two were together before. I thought you were both young. Too young to be making adult decisions like marriage and family and entering the Marines." She smiled, but it shook and disappeared quickly. "But you're a good mom. And you've done good things with your life. I'm proud of you."

Tears ran down her face, and she hurried toward Alice and drew her into a hug. Alice couldn't help crying with her mother for a minute. "Thanks, Mom."

"I'm assuming Hunter has grown and matured too," she said, stepping back. "So." She straightened he shoulders. "I'm willing to give him a second chance. And help him with whatever he needs so he can be a father for Westin."

"Thank you, Mom," Alice whispered.

"And who knows?" her mom asked. "Maybe you and Hunter can be the family you've always dreamed you could be."

"Mom." Alice shook her head. "I don't know about that. Don't hope for that."

"Why not?" her mom asked. "You are."

"I am not."

Her mom smiled and cradled Alice's face I her hand. "It's okay to hope for that," she said. "Then you'd have everything the nineteen-year-old you assured me you'd have. And." She lifted her eyebrows and gave her a knowing look. "Don't think I don't know that you haven't dated anyone since Hunter. And there have been plenty of opportunities."

Heat rose to Alice's face, and she looked out the window. "I'm not interested in dating." Her mother didn't argue with her, thankfully. And besides, Alice had spoken true. She wasn't interested in dating...unless the man across the table was Hunter Magleby.

9

Hunter sat in front of his new laptop, searching for jobs here in Hawthorne Harbor. He'd gotten some decent technology training in the Marines, and he thought he could handle an office job part-time.

He looked through the few jobs there were, but he didn't meet any of the requirements. No degree. No experience with certain programs. And he had no idea how fast he could type.

Frustrated, he closed the computer and leaned back, his gaze wandering out the window and then to the clock. Westin would be coming that night, and Alice was bringing pizza, his backpack and homework, and his pillow with them.

Nerves ran through him at the speed of light, and his heartbeat responded to the spike in adrenaline. He'd spent some time with Westin over the past week, but only a few minutes, and never alone.

What was he going to do with Westin for hours before bedtime? Outside, a car door slammed, and Clara raised her head from the floor at his feet.

"Get the door," he said, but she just cocked her head. "Answer it," he tried again.

Clara got up and went over to the front door, opening it before another car door slammed. Hunter heard Westin's pretend shooting noises before he saw the boy burst into the house.

"Hey, buddy." He planted both palms flat on the desk and pushed himself to a standing position.

"Dad," Westin said, and the word seemed to echo through him endlessly. He was a dad. The boy in front of him was his son. "Mom got pizza, and I only like pepperoni. She said you liked pepperoni too, so she said it would be okay."

"It's fine," Hunter said, smiling. "I like pepperoni pizza just fine."

Alice came through the doorway, holding two boxes of pizza. "Westin, you left your backpack in the car. Go get it, please."

"He said pepperoni was fine."

"I told you," she said to the little boy as he skipped out to the porch. Alice smiled at his retreating back and then looked at Hunter. "I brought the cheeseburger supreme too." She lifted the boxes, and for a moment, Hunter thought he could cross the room quickly and take them from her.

He took a step before he remembered that he couldn't do that. That he shouldn't be walking without his cane at all. He threw his hand out and steadied himself on the desk. "You can put them in the kitchen," he said, a dose of humiliation splashing his insides.

Alice moved easily, the way most people did, and set the boxes on the kitchen counter. Her fingers wound around and around one another. Hunter stayed where he was and waited for her to find the courage to say what was on her mind.

He'd seen her do this a few times before. He imagined that when she'd gotten their marriage annulled and then emailed him about it, that she'd twisted her fingers around each other like this. It was something she always did when she was nervous, and it was comforting to know some things hadn't changed about her.

Of course, other things had absolutely changed, and Hunter was glad that she was wiser now. Responsible and hard-working. And still so beautiful. He drew in a deep breath through his nose and employed his patience.

"Okay, so you're his father, and you can do what you want. But he does have to go to school in the morning, and his teacher has to deal with him."

"You want me to put him to bed on time."

"He does have a bedtime." She turned back to the

pizza boxes and plucked a sheet of paper off the top of them. "I made you a cheat sheet."

Hunter wasn't sure if he should be thankful or offended. He quickly decided on grateful, because he really didn't know how to take care of an eight-year-old. He thought he'd probably have felt this level of panic and insecurity on the day they brought Westin home from the hospital, but of course, he'd missed that day.

Alice rattled the paper, and Hunter realized he'd disappeared into his mind for a moment. He took the paper and glanced at it. It was a skeleton schedule, and Hunter smiled at Alice's attention to detail.

"You always were so organized," he said.

"Thank you."

Westin skipped back into the room, a Spiderman backpack hanging on one shoulder. "I don't have any homework."

"Your dad will check anyway," Alice said, stepping over to him and gathering Westin into a tight hug. "You be good for him, okay?"

"Okay, Mama." Westin seemed happy about everything, and he seemed to be able to adapt to all kinds of changes in a single heartbeat. Hunter used to live like that—until the brutalities of war and combat had hardened him. Made him crave normalcy and a schedule.

Alice nodded, and the pained, panicked look in her eyes told him that leaving Westin here was very difficult for her. Hunter wondered if she had this same level of anxiety when she dropped Westin at her mother's, but he had no way of knowing.

And he'd have to deal with Karen tomorrow morning. Alice had said her mom was okay with Hunter taking Westin in the evenings.

"Alice?" he asked as she stepped onto the porch. He grabbed his cane and started after her, hoping for a little distance between her and Westin.

"Yeah?"

He hobbled over to her. "I, uh, haven't gotten a picture from you today."

Surprise entered her eyes, and she blinked and fell back a step. "You're right. I'll send it right now."

"I...." Hunter looked over his shoulder where Westin had dropped his backpack on the couch and then sat next to it. He held the remote in his hand and was pushing buttons on it as the TV changed channels.

Hunter looked back at Alice. "I really like the pictures, Alice."

"I'm glad." She smiled. "I wasn't sure how to...you know." She wiped her hand through her hand and sighed. "I'm sorry, Hunter. I'm trying."

"You're doing great," he said, unsure of what she was trying and felt like she was failing at.

"I'll keep sending the pictures." She nodded and acted like she'd leave again.

Hunter reached out and touched her arm. Fireworks exploded from his fingertips and up into his elbow. He pulled his hand back quickly, but the heat remained in his skin. "I'd like...." He wasn't sure how to finish.

Just ask her out.

He'd had to work himself up to asking her out a decade ago too. Why was it just as hard this time? He'd married this woman.

"Maybe we could go to, I don't know. Lunch? Coffee?"

Alice's eyes widened, the shock evident. "Are you asking me out?"

Hunter wanted to deny it, but instead he squared his shoulders and said, "Yes, Alice. I'm asking you out."

A slow smile spread across her face, and she giggled as she tucked her hair behind her ear. "All right, Hunter. I'll go out with you on one condition."

"Oh, yeah?" he asked, enjoying this game and feeling strangely like they'd played it before. "What's that?"

She plucked her keys from her pocket and jangled them. "I get to drive." With that, she walked away. She'd reached the bottom of the steps when Hunter started laughing, and it felt really nice to have happiness bubbling up inside him.

He turned back to the house, walked inside, and closed the door behind him. "All right, bud," he said, looking at the paper. "This says we have to eat and do homework. Bath tonight, and in bed by eight-thirty." He looked at Westin. "So let's eat."

Westin went over to the kitchen table, where Hunter moved the pizza boxes. They ate without plates while

Westin told him about his friend at school who had a pet lizard.

"I have a hedgehog, so I guess it's good too."

"You have a pet hedgehog?" Hunter asked.

"Yeah," his son said.

"Who takes care of it overnight? Do you have to feed it in the morning?"

"Mom will, when she gets home," Westin said, unconcerned.

"Lucky," Hunter said, "I have to take care of Clara all the time, and I don't have a mom to help me."

"I bet my mom would help you." Westin looked at him with such innocence in his eyes. Hunter didn't know what to say, so he took another bite of his pizza.

"She's really good with dogs," he continued as if Hunter had never met Alice before. "She's not great with throwing a ball or anything like that. But all the kids at the hospital like her, and she goes to the animal shelter every...I don't know. We go every few weeks."

Hunter's eyebrows went up. "Your mom goes to the animal shelter? And does what?"

"I don't know."

"Does she get paid?"

"I don't know."

Hunter was almost certain she didn't get paid. So she volunteered at the animal shelter. Fascinating. He did not remember her being overly enthusiastic about dogs and cats when they'd been together before.

"I can throw you a ball," he said next, hoping he could find the right balance on his bad leg to actually do something like that.

"Yeah?" Westin's face brightened again. "Right now?"

"It's dark," Hunter said.

"Not quite." Westin tossed down his partially eaten piece of pizza and jumped up, the chair scraping the tile as it flew backward. "I brought my mitt."

"I don't have one," Hunter said, but he could catch without one. He abandoned his food too, thinking there was plenty of time to eat later. If his son wanted to throw a ball right now, in the last rays of the day's light, Hunter was going to do that.

He stood and took precious seconds to find his balance and grip his cane while Westin dug in his backpack for his glove. He smacked the ball in the leather and said, "You ready, Dad?"

Dad.

Hunter grinned at him. "I'm ready, bud." He nodded toward the back door and said, "You want Clara to open it?"

"She can open the door?" Westin seemed to find so much joy in absolutely everything, even the simplest of things.

"She sure can." Hunter looked down at Clara. "Clara, answer it." He pointed to the back door. "That one. Answer it."

Clara got up and clicked over to the back door and

opened it. She turned and looked over her shoulder with a grin on her face.

"Wow," Westin said. "She's the best dog ever." He skipped over to her and buried his face in her fur. "You're so great, Clara." Then he went outside, his boyish voice singing something that made Hunter's heart soar.

He followed his son outside at a much slower pace and positioned himself on the flat, solid, dirt-packed ground while Westin chose a spot of grass. "All right," he called and clapped his hands. "Right here, Westie."

The nickname just rolled off Hunter's tongue, and he marveled at how easy it was to be with his son, though the boy was essentially a complete stranger. Westin threw the ball, and it didn't come quite close enough for Hunter to catch.

Westin certainly wasn't going to be a professional baseball player, but he darted forward and collected the ball, underhanding it to Hunter before dashing back to the lawn. "All right, Dad. I'm ready."

Hunter lobbed the ball to Westin, happiness filling him from head to toe that he could still do this simple thing with his son. Westin caught the ball easily and cocked his arm to throw it back.

Once again, the ball went in a wildly different direction than Westin intended it to, and the sharp crack of breaking glass filled the air. Clara barked from her spot a few feet from Hunter—always only a few feet from Hunter.

"Oh, no," Westin moaned, but Hunter started laughing. Clara barked again, and Hunter quieted.

"It's fine," he said to Westin.

"You're not mad?" his son asked as he walked closer.

"It's a window," Hunter said. "It's replaceable." Unlike his hip, knee, and ankle.

Westin looked at how heavily Hunter leaned on his cane. "What happened to your leg, Dad?"

Hunter blew out his breath and turned toward the steps. He sat on the third one from the bottom so he could stretch his legs out straight. "I got hit while I was on my ship," he said. "Kind of like a big car accident." Not like that at all, but he didn't want to scare Westin. He knew words like "bombing" and "explosion" were scary, because he'd lived through them.

He took a breath, smelling the acrid, burning scent of diesel fuel for a moment. It was strange how his mind recalled the smallest details from the accident.

"And my leg got pinned up against one of our tanks and got damaged. That's why I came home." He regretted his last words as soon as they left his mouth. "I mean...I was going to retire in a few years anyway, but after I got injured, I decided I was done in the Marines."

And that wasn't really his choice.

"What did you do on the tank?" Westin asked.

"I was part of a Marine Expeditionary Unit," Hunter said, his memories of his friends and battalion mates as strong as the weight of the tank against his right leg. "I was on an amphibious ship, and we did all kinds of things. We were escorting a submarine that had a high threat on it when the accident happened."

He'd seen water burn before, in videos and training exercises. He'd never been in the midst of it, wondering if anyone would ever find his remains at the bottom of the ocean. And it had been much scarier in real life than in the videos.

He blinked the blue and orange pictures in his mind disappearing. "I better go clean up that glass. That's my bedroom." He pushed himself to his feet and looked at Westin. "You want to walk down to my cousin's place after? They have an eight-year-old boy named Porter."

"Porter Baker?" Westin asked, the heavier topic not staying with him for long.

"Yeah," Hunter said. "You know him?"

"Yeah." He jumped to his feet and bounced on the balls of his feet. "Porter's in my class."

"Well, great. You go on ahead with Clara if you want. I'll clean up and come down." He went up the steps slowly, a bit startled to see Westin coming with him.

"I'll help you," Westin said. "I broke the window, and you shouldn't have to clean it up."

Hunter smiled at him and, acting on an impulse, he gathered his son into a hug and said, "I love you, buddy."

His son's shoulders shook and he said, "I love you too, Dad. I'm glad your accident wasn't too bad."

Hunter couldn't say anything else, because the lump

in his throat prevented his vocal cords from working. But he decided that he was going to try to have the outlook on life that his son did.

I'm alive.

I have a good house to live in. A great dog. An amazing son. And a date with Alice.

Oh, yes, Hunter had plenty to smile about.

Alice had one of the worst shifts of her career. Doctor Bear was back, and he seemed even more growly than usual. Leaving Westin at Hunter's had put her on-edge, especially when she'd gotten a text from him that said, *Hey Mom! This is Westin. Dad let me borrow his phone. We're having so much fun!*

Of course she wanted her son to have fun with Hunter. She was glad about that. She just hoped Westin wasn't wearing Hunter to the bone. The man had a major injury and by his own admission, didn't do much more than sit in a recliner and train his dog.

She made it through her shift and smiled at the picture Hunter had sent of Westin with Porter Baker, who lived just down the road. An iota of her guilt lifted when she realized that Hunter was getting some time with his son. Time to make memories and learn about him.

She sat in her driveway and sent him another picture of Westin as a baby. He loved Tupperware, she typed out. Got it out of the cupboard every day and banged it together or on the ground. I just left it out for him all day, cleaned it up at night, and let him do it all over again the next day.

She smiled at the memory from Westin's babyhood—a time of her life when she'd wondered if she'd ever feel happy again. Some days, she lied to herself and made up fantasies about her husband off on a long business trip. That was why she was alone with her baby son all day long. Alone.

Not because she'd panicked the moment he'd left town and driven two hours to get the marriage annulled. Not because she'd succumbed to the pressure from her parents.

And when she'd then discovered she was pregnant, the marriage was already over. Hunter had already been notified—and he hadn't responded. Everything was done.

Regret lanced through her, but it wasn't as sharp as it had once been. She wasn't sure why, but she was relieved she didn't have to live in constant fear anymore.

Not only that, but Hunter had asked her out.

Warmth started down in her toes, and she realized how chilly she was. Her car's heater had stopped blowing warm air again, because she wasn't actively driving. She twisted the key and turned off the engine before heading inside, where thankfully, her furnace worked.

She couldn't help glancing at the clock and noting that her mother should've picked up Westin twenty minutes ago to take him to school. *Please let everything have gone well*, she thought.

Could she text her mom and find out? Hunter?

In the end, she decided not to do either and instead, went to bed as she normally did. After all, she hardly ever texted her mom to make sure Westin got to school on other days.

When she woke, her mouth felt like something had crawled inside and died. Her jaw ached, because she ground her teeth while she slept.

She opened her mouth wide and went to brush her teeth. She'd woken before her alarm by ten minutes, so by the time she showered and was ready, she had a few spare minutes to swing through the drive-through at Drinks and Donuts, her favorite coffee hotspot on the way to the elementary school.

Plus, if she sugared Westin up with doughnuts and hot chocolate, he'd be more likely to tell her everything that had happened since she'd seen him last.

He opened the car door, breaking into her thoughts and startling her. "Hey," she said, reaching for her seatbelt again.

"Hey, Mom." He climbed in the car and buckled in too. He immediately started digging into his sack lunch, which looked like it was still full.

"You didn't eat lunch?" she asked as she inched forward in the pick-up line.

"I did. It was chicken fried steak and mashed potatoes today." He pulled out a granola bar—the kind Alice never bought because they were more chocolate than granola. "But Dad packed me this, and I don't want him to feel bad that I didn't eat it."

"You don't have to eat it," Alice said. "He'll never know." She hated those words, and she couldn't believe she'd said them. "I mean—"

"He'll know," Westin said. "He knows *everything*, Mom."

Alice quirked her eyebrows at Westin. "He does? What makes you say that?"

"Porter's mom was having a problem with something on the computer, and Dad sat right down and fixed it. Then one of the new dogs started going crazy, and Dad hushed her. Trent said Hunter should work with him on training the dogs."

Alice's fingers tightened on the steering wheel. "That doesn't sound like everything, bud."

"He made eggs this morning just how I like them, and he had chocolate milk."

Alice suppressed a sigh. "Were you good at school?" She looked at Westin out of the corner of her eye. She didn't like to accuse him of anything, but if he got chocolate milk or sugary cereal in the morning, he went to school a bit wired. His poor teacher....

"I was good," he said. "I got to yellow before recess, but I worked back to green."

"Good boy," she said with a smile. "Homework tonight?"

"Dad said he'd help me with it." Westin finished the granola bar and turned toward her. "Mom, were you and Dad married?"

A blast of heat moved through her. "Yes," she said. "For a brief time."

"Because my friend Davy says you can't have a baby if you're not married."

Well, that wasn't entirely accurate, but Alice wasn't going to correct the thinking quite yet. "Dad and I were married. He was deployed when you were born."

"And you got divorced." This time, it wasn't a question.

"Yes—well, no...." Alice felt like she'd been trapped, painted into a corner. How did she answer this question? How could she explain an annulment to her eight-year-old?

"No? So you're still married?"

"No, Westie. We're not married anymore." A bolt of sadness struck her, and Alice wished she hadn't been quite so young when she'd made so many life decisions. "I had the marriage annulled. What that means is basically, I asked the judge to say we were never married. And he did."

Westin didn't say anything, and Alice let his little mind

stew on whatever it needed to. She pulled in the driveway at home and said, "Spaghetti tonight?"

"Dad said if you'd come get him, we could go to that noodle buffet."

"Noodle buffet?" Alice asked, killing the engine and getting out of the car.

Westin dragged his backpack around the car. "Yeah. With the pizza and salad bar and all the noodles and sauces. He said then you won't have to cook. He said you don't like cooking."

"I can cook," she said defensively. Hadn't she made Hunter homemade chicken noodle soup? With *homemade* pasta? Yes. Yes, she had.

"He said...." Westin continued talking, but Alice tuned him out. If her son said, "He said," one more time, she might lose her mind. Had Hunter stayed up all night talking to Westin? Jeez, when had he had time to say all these things?

Alice washed the dishes while Westin got out his toy cars. He made an assortment of vrooming noises and carried on entire conversations with himself while she puttered around the kitchen, not really doing anything.

After all, she hadn't made dinner the night before, and her breakfast and lunch had consisted of air. With the coffee, she'd be good until that evening—unless they were really going to Pizza Pipeline for an all-she-could-eat buffet of pizza, pasta, and salad.

She leaned against the counter and texted Hunter. *We're going to dinner tonight? With Westin?*

If you'd like, his response came almost immediately. She could just see him casually looking out the window as he spoke the words, his voice deep and rich and wonderful, making her soul vibrate as if it were made of guitar strings and he'd just plucked them.

Is this the date? she asked, hoping her fun, flirty feelings came through in the text. But she knew they didn't. Even a decade ago, Hunter had been more of a fan of stopping by her parents' house in the dead of night so they could talk instead of text.

But he didn't have a car now, and he wouldn't be showing up at her place to tap on her window from the branch in the tree he'd climbed.

He couldn't climb trees now. Her heart pinched and twisted in her chest. He hadn't told her how he'd been injured, and she knew he carried more than the physical scars on his right leg. Maybe, if they kept communicating and seeing each other, she'd learn everything about him again.

His text finally came in and it said, No. Taking our son doesn't count as a date.

Our son. The words blurred in her vision, no matter how many times she blinked.

So what would you call this? She grinned at the phone as she imagined Hunter sitting in his house, trying to figure out how to answer her questions.

A meal you don't have to make, he sent back. Or clean up after.

Ah, so he knew how to go right to her heart. Of course, Hunter always had, even if he didn't know it.

Plus, maybe I want to see you for more than five minutes.

Alice's heart tippity-tapped in her chest, and now she was the one with no idea how to respond. Her thumbs hovered over the letters, but she didn't move a muscle.

"Mom," Westin said.

"Huh? What?" She almost dropped her phone as she spun toward him. She'd forgotten all about him as she flirted with the boy's father.

"I asked if we could go with Dad to the noodle buffet." He ran one of his cars along the countertop, the scratching of the wheels grating against Alice's nerves.

"Yeah," she said. "I was just talking to him about it." She shoved her phone in her pocket though it buzzed with another message. *Could be from anyone*, she told herself. It didn't have to be Hunter.

But she didn't pull it out and check, because she was doing a lot more than talking to Hunter. She was fantasizing about him again. What it would be like to kiss him now that he was more man than boy. More muscle than macho. More wise than worried.

Her face heated, and she tucked her hair behind her ear. "You want to do a puzzle?" That would keep her mind off Hunter.

"Yeah, let's work on that gumball one." He danced ahead of her to one of two folding tables set up in the dining room. They ate at the kitchen counter most nights, or she grabbed something on her way to her mother's, or her parents fed Westin.

One of the tables had two puzzles on it, with a carefully placed line of masking tape down the middle to keep the pieces separate. The other table held the gumball puzzle, which was a thousand pieces, with flat colors that could go anywhere. Dozens of blue, pink, yellow, red, white, and green gumballs filled the machine, and it was literally like trying one piece at a time until one went in.

Sometimes she and Westin sat down to work on this puzzle and didn't place a single piece. She hoped today they'd be able to at least put together something.

She sighed as she eased into the chair in front of the window. Westin perched on the other chair, already studying the pieces. She took a moment to study him, that flop of dark hair, the sharp slope of his nose that echoed his father's. He really had been a beautiful baby, and the cutest little boy in the world. She'd kept his hair shaved short in the summer, and she missed those buzz cuts.

Before she even looked at a piece, she opened her gallery on her phone and found one of the pictures of Westin with that shorn hair. It wasn't the picture Hunter was supposed to get today—in fact, he'd already gotten his Picture of the Day.

But she couldn't help herself. Westin was the cutest little boy. I loved buzzing his hair in the summer.

She sent the text and read his other message. He'd asked *Do you want to see me for more than five minutes?*

She was just tapping out *Oh, I do* when she caught Westin looking at her. "We're working on the puzzle," he said pointedly.

"I was just talking to Dad."

"Let's send him a picture of us," Westin said with a grin. He came around the table and smashed the side of his face against hers in perfect selfie-taking fashion.

She giggled and held up her phone to snap the shot.

"Wait, wait," he said, grabbing a piece of the puzzle. "I want it to have a puzzle piece in it. Can you ask him if he likes puzzles?"

"I'm surprised you didn't talk about that last night," Alice said, positioning the phone for another picture. She took it, and Westin walked back to his place across from her. He obviously hadn't heard her sarcasm, and she was grateful. She wouldn't know how to explain anyway.

She sent the picture to Hunter with Westin's question and focused on the puzzle. But she put her phone face-up beside her, something she never did. So she saw Hunter's text when it came in.

I love it!

Alice warmed at his words. And she wondered if one of them—that tiny two-letter word—could be changed to a different, three-letter one.

I love you.

"He's waiting for us," Alice said as her headlights cut a path of light across Hunter's porch. He stood at the bottom of the steps, all ready to go. "Stay here."

She got out of the car, noticing the way the engine clicked. Hunter obviously heard it too, because he frowned at the hood.

"I can look at that for you," he said.

"When are you going to do that?" she asked, completely forgetting what she was going to say instead. But it surely was something fun and flirty, not confrontational.

"I don't have a job yet," he said coolly. "I can come over while you sleep."

She wanted to ask how he'd get there, but she didn't want to insult him.

"You could pick me up on your way home from the hospital," he said. "And I'll look at it."

Having him at her house would ensure she'd never be able to fall asleep. Nerves assaulted her stomach just thinking about it. So she said nothing, her mind whirring as fast as her emotions.

He limped over to the passenger door, and she sprang into motion, moving to help him. He glared at her, and she felt like his eyes had burned her.

"Sorry, I was just trying to help."

"I don't need help opening the door," he said, his voice almost a growl. She'd heard him make that noise before, and it had lit more of a fire in her belly than it did now.

"How late was Westin up last night?" she asked, unsure of why she was asking.

"He went to bed at the time you listed on that cheat sheet."

She stood partway between him and the door, and she didn't move.

"Are we going or not?" he asked. "It's not exactly warm out here."

"I'm sorry," she blurted.

He cocked his head. "For what, Alice?"

"For not telling you."

"We already talked about that."

"Sort of," she said.

"And you want to go more in-depth now?" He glanced to the back seat, but Westin had obediently stayed like Alice had asked.

"I just want you to know."

"Well," he said, taking a half-step closer to her and putting his hand on hers, which still rested on the door handle. "If you want to feel sorry, you can. But it should be for the right things."

"What things?" she asked, hoping that if he told her, she'd be able to make them up to him.

"For not including me," he said, his voice a bit rough

around the edges. "I just want to belong somewhere, with someone. And that could've been you and Westin for a lot of years." He pulled on the door and opened it, stepping around it to put it between them and sinking into the seat. "Hey, bud," she heard before she turned away, her lungs searing with shame.

11

Hunter hadn't intended to hurt Alice's feelings that night. But she'd stood there, looking at him with such fire in her eyes. Her apology had been genuine, but Hunter knew she didn't even know what she was apologizing for.

She might as well know, he told himself as she went down to the end of the lane and turned around.

"Porter lives there, Mom," Westin said from the back seat, oblivious to the tension between the adults up front.

"Yeah," Alice said, her voice a bit on the high side.

"How was school?" he asked Westin.

"Great," Westin said, launching into a story about the mashed potato tower he sculpted at lunch. "But I ate your lunch after school, Dad."

Hunter smiled at him in the rear-view mirror. "If you want to eat school lunch, that's fine."

"Just some days," Alice said, glancing at him. "There's a schedule online."

"I'll look that up," Hunter said, foolishness blipping through him in time with his pulse. He didn't need to be making peanut butter sandwiches if Westin wasn't going to eat them.

"Dad, tonight can we throw the ball again?"

"It's already dark, bud."

"I hate winter," he complained, and Hunter chuckled.

"Me too, kid." He had prayed for winter, though, when he'd been assigned a mission in the desert, sweating his skin off. Sand everywhere. No air conditioning. "Maybe your Mom could bring you over earlier tomorrow," he said carefully. He didn't want to take all of Westin's time outside of school. "We could throw the ball then, as long as you don't break another window." He grinned at Westin as Alice inhaled sharply.

"Westin," she said. "You broke a window?"

"It was an accident," Hunter said at the same time as Westin. They both looked at Alice, who steadfastly stared out the windshield.

"I'll pay you back," Alice said.

"That's not necessary," Hunter said, wishing he could reach across the gearshift between them and take her hand in his. "It was no big deal. Trent took me to the hardware store, and I did it myself this afternoon."

"Still," she said.

"Alice," he said, ready to die on this hill. "He's my son too."

"I know that," she snapped, finally removing her eyes from the empty road in front of them to glare at Hunter.

Hunter held fast, barely blinking at the harshness in her voice. "I'm simply saying that if you and I...I mean, if we...he's my son, and it was an accident. I don't need you to pay for it." Heat filled him, and he was suddenly glad for the wintry temperatures closer to the glass. He leaned his head against it and breathed in deep, deeper.

"Did you get any of that puzzle done?" he asked, hoping they could just move past this, the same way he could forget about her jumping out of the car to help him. He'd hurt his leg, not his hands, and he could open the blasted door himself.

Yes, he'd descended the steps fifteen minutes before her set arrival time. He didn't want to be watched doing that. But he could open a car door.

Westin talked about the puzzle for a moment, and then the silence returned.

"How did things go with my mother this morning?" Alice asked next, and Hunter lifted his head, determined not to show his exhaustion.

"Great," he said, and his tone was false to his own ears.

"She honked," Westin said. "Dad didn't like that."

"Westin," he said. "That was our secret, remember?"

"Yeah," Westin said.

"But you just told Mom." He twisted, the movement

pulling in his hip strangely. He hurried to turn back to the front.

"Oh, sorry," Westin said.

"I'll tell her not to honk," Alice said.

"Please don't do that," Hunter said. "It was fine. Westin was fed and dressed and ready."

Alice pulled into the restaurant parking lot, and she turned back to Westin. "Go say hi to Tammy, okay, bud? I want to talk to Dad for a minute." Her eyes caught on Hunter's, and his mind went into overdrive. He wanted to say all kinds of soft things to her, but by the edge in her eye, that wasn't what she was going to say.

"All right," he said. "Can I have the candy she gives me?"

"Yep," Alice said, watching him while he climbed out of the car and walked into the restaurant. Only then did she look at Hunter.

He looked right back. He sure had enjoyed looking at her previously. That long, dark hair. Her porcelain complexion. Those full lips.... His heart pinballed in his chest, and all he could think about was kissing her.

"I'm sorry about my mother."

"Don't be sorry about things you can't control," he said.

"I'm sorry I didn't include you."

Hunter swallowed, because he didn't want to bear his entire soul to her. The little he'd said had been enough. If he did, he'd be opening the door all the way for her.

Haven't you already? he asked himself. He'd asked her out. Told her he wanted to see her for more than five minutes. Asked her if she wanted to see him too—a question she'd never answered.

He couldn't believe he was even entertaining ideas about the two of them.

"The pictures help," he said, the honesty raw in his voice. "He really was a cute little boy."

"He's still a little boy, Hunter."

"Yeah." He gazed at the restaurant windows, glowing with yellow light in this winter night.

Alice's hand was cool when it touched his, and her fingers seemed to be able snake right in between his without any resistance. He sighed and leaned his head back. "You never said if you wanted to see me for more than five minutes."

"I didn't think I needed to," she whispered.

"Oh?" He looked at her, seeing her apprehension even through the dim light.

"I never had to spell out how I felt about you before," she said.

"Well, things change," he said.

"Yes." She nodded. "They sure do." She sighed and added, "We better go in. Tammy will kill me if I leave Westin in there alone for too long. Then she'll ask me all kinds of awkward questions about you." She threw him a flirty smile and got out of the car.

Hunter did too, taking substantially longer than she

did. She waited for him at the front of the car, and she tucked her arm through his elbow as they walked toward the restaurant. Panic hit him full in the chest when he walked in and realized it was only a buffet. He'd thought he could order something too, and Westin could still get all the noodles he wanted.

Buffets meant he had to carry something in one hand and try to walk with his cane with the other. The tension in his chest and shoulders felt akin to cracking.

He could do this. He'd thrown a ball to his son. He'd served him pizza. He could put some food on a plate and carry it to a table. He certainly wasn't going to let Alice or Westin do it for him.

It took him longer than them, but he got the job done. Finally all in the booth together, he said, "So I think I might have found a job."

"Oh, yeah?" Alice asked. "Doing what?"

"My cousin owns a construction firm. She needs someone to run the office. Lauren's doing more and more at the Magleby Mansion, and she can't keep up with the accounts and jobs anymore like she used to." He took a drink of his soda. "It's a desk job. Computers. I'm good with computers."

"That's great, Dad," Westin said, looking at Alice. "I told you he fixed something on her computer."

"Oh, have you been talking about me?" he asked Westin, plenty of teasing in his voice.

"He wouldn't shut up about you," Alice said dryly, and

Hunter laughed. Alice smiled at least, so that was good, and the new silence that enveloped them felt wonderful and comfortable.

Hunter did feel like he belonged with these people— his family. And it had been such a long time since he'd felt like that, like he had a true family that would be beside him through thick and thin.

Yes, his battalion had been like family. As much as a group of men could feel like a family. To Hunter, they'd been important, but it was nothing like truly belonging to someone and having them belong to you.

He'd been in love with Alice once. Deep down, he still loved her. That feeling had a long way to go before it reached the surface, but for now, just knowing it was there —dormant and buried, but there—was enough.

HUNTER WOKE THE NEXT MORNING WITH AN ACHE IN BOTH hips. Odd, but not completely new. Sometimes his good hip overcompensated for the weaker one, and he kept a bottle of painkillers in his nightstand just in case he needed them before he got out of bed.

Today was one of those days, and he swallowed two pills dry and laid there for another twenty minutes before getting up to let Clara outside.

Westin was already awake, sitting at the table in his pajamas, a tablet on the table in front of him.

"Hey, bud," Hunter said. "Are we eating home lunch or school lunch today?"

"I'll look it up," Westin said.

After dinner last night, he and Westin had done his homework, and then they'd played a game on his tablet before he'd gone to bed. Hunter had enjoyed himself immensely, and he was starting to think that if he could find a way through the maze of his emotions to where he could forgive Alice, they might be able to become the family they should've been for the past eight years.

An unexpected wave of bitterness engulfed him, and he started brewing coffee while his son tapped and swiped on his tablet to check the lunch schedule.

"Home lunch," he finally said. "And can I have some of that cereal in the cupboard?"

A scratch came on the back door, and Hunter hobbled over to it to let Clara in. "Cereal, yes. Home lunch, on it." He poured Westin a bowl of the brightly colored loops and set to work putting together a lunch.

"Go get dressed," he said once Westin finished eating. "Your grandmother will be here soon."

A horn blared in the next moment, and Hunter's eyes flew to the clock. "Hurry, bud. She's here already."

She was a few minutes early, but they'd been ready by this time yesterday. Worry ran through him, but he tamed it and hurried to finish folding the flap on the brown paper bag and scrawling Westin's name on it.

"Where's your backpack?" he called, glancing around

the living room. He'd definitely had it last night, as he'd pulled his math worksheets out of it. But Hunter didn't see it now.

Another blast from the horn had his irritation through the roof. "Answer it," he said to Clara, who didn't seem upset at all as she went to open the door. Hunter still couldn't find Westin's backpack, and he gave up the search in favor of moving over to the door and holding up one finger to say she could wait.

Alice's mother got out of the car, her lips pursed. She'd looked at Hunter like that so often, he thought she must have a mask she put on before she saw him. Karen tapped her wrist, but Hunter didn't care if the boy was late for third grade.

It was *third grade*, not a college entrance exam.

"Come in," he called, hoping maybe she could spot the elusive backpack or help Westin get ready faster.

Karen did not look happy as she approached the steps. Hunter turned and went back inside, catching sight of the Spiderman backpack on the coat hooks. He grabbed it and unzipped the top to put in Westin's lunch.

He'd mentioned to Alice about having her come and pick him up after her shift, but they'd never come back to that conversation. He wasn't going to ask her mother for a ride, that was dang sure.

"Sorry," he said when she stepped through the door. He wouldn't qualify his apology. She didn't need to know that his hips hurt that morning and it had taken him longer to get out of bed than usual. "Westin," he called. "How's it going?"

"I can't find my shoes."

"They're out here." Hunter nudged them with his foot when Westin came into the living room.

"Hey, Grandma," he said, utterly nonplussed at the double horn-honk and laser-eyed look.

"We're going to be late, Westie," she said.

He shoved his feet in his still-tied shoes while she lectured him about untying them first. Hunter handed him the backpack and said, "Your lunch is in there, bud. See you tonight."

"Bye, Dad." Westin wrapped his arms around Hunter and squeezed. For a boy so small and wiry, he sure was strong.

Hunter bent down and kissed the top of his son's head before he let go, and Westin moved over to Karen and took her hand.

She didn't move though. She continued to stare at Hunter, something changing in her expression right before his eyes. She finally nodded, turned, and left with Westin.

Hunter moved over to the doorframe and leaned his good side into it so his injured leg could get a break. "Bye, Westie," he said softly to the cold morning. "I love you."

Karen drove away, the sound of her car finally fading back to silence before Hunter went inside and closed the door. "All right, Clara," he said. "We're going for a walk. Let me get my shoes."

Forgotten Road sat too far from town to really walk anywhere, but he went to the main road and then all the way down the lane past Lauren's house. Back and forth, Clara running ahead or sniffing something behind, always coming back to his side whenever he whistled.

By the time he got back to his house, he was tired both mentally and physically.

"I like Alice," he said. "Despite what she's done, I like her."

Yes, he'd asked her out. Held her hand briefly. But he liked to acknowledge things, recognize them out loud, before really committing to them.

"I like her," he said again, the words feeling nice and whole coming from his mouth.

Now he just had to figure out how to trust her again.

12

Alice was considering a career change by the time the week was over. Dr. Murphy had disappeared from the face of the planet, and Dr. Bear—er, Scoville—made the graveyard shift almost unbearable.

She scoffed at the word un*bear*able.

But she'd survived another week, and she had Sunday and Monday off. She wanted to sleep until she woke naturally. No alarm. No rushing to get over to the school to pick up Westin.

And she could have that luxury, because Hunter had Westin for the weekend.

Alice was getting better at filling her time with her own wants, and it hadn't taken long for her to do so. Westin had been going to Hunter's for a couple of weeks now, and it seemed like everyone had settled into a nice rhythm.

Her mother had said nothing about the exchanges with Hunter in the morning, and neither had he. The one time she'd asked Westin, her son had said, "It's fine, Mom."

Hunter could've said those words, and Alice had wanted to argue with Westin. Tell him he could be honest with her. At the same time, he was right. No one had said anything, so as far as Alice knew, everything was fine.

She hated feeling like she was stuck in the middle, though. She wasn't sure why her mother couldn't forgive Hunter and see that he'd changed.

She finally gave up on sleeping and rolled into a sitting position. Feeling very lazy and completely scattered, she reached for her phone. She had a few messages from Hunter, each one accelerating her pulse.

Morning, beautiful.

I hope you got to sleep as long as you wanted.

I asked your mother to take Westin this afternoon, because I thought you and I could have our date.

She's dropping me off about four. I hope you're ready to drive.

Alice could not find what time it was fast enough. After working four twelve-hour shifts, three right in a row, she had been bone-tired.

And now it was three-thirty.

She had thirty minutes to make herself presentable enough for a date. Yet she sat frozen, trying to decide what to do. Shower? Her hair would be wet, and there'd be no way to get it dry fast enough.

Or go with the casual, just-rolled-out-of-bed look? She could pile her hair on top of her head in a messy bun and spend the other twenty-five minutes perfecting her makeup and obsessing over what kind of outfit she should wear.

So no shower.

She took a few seconds to tap out a response for him, saying four o'clock was fine, and then she flew into motion.

Hunter had never been the pretentious type. He wouldn't take her somewhere fancy, so she didn't need to dress up. But maybe she wanted to.

She stood in her tiny walk-in closet and stared at the array of clothing there. She had a few dresses she wore to church, or leftover from a fancy hospital party or a brides-maid dress for a now-distant friend.

But really, in the winter, she loved wearing jeans and sweaters when she wasn't working. So she pulled out a dark park of jeans and a sweat the color of brown mustard, and went to work on her face. She still had lines from her pillow pressed into her cheek, for crying out loud.

Her mind flew through the destinations Hunter might have in mind. *I hope you're ready to drive.*

What did that mean? Bell Hill was twenty-five minutes away, hardly a long drive. They could go up to

Seattle, but that was a two-hour drive. Had he arranged for Westin to sleep over at her parents'? What had he told them?

By the time she slicked on her deep purple lip gloss and deemed herself ready, her anxiety levels had reached a new peak.

And then someone knocked on the door.

Not someone. Hunter.

She smoothed her palms down her sweater and went to answer the door. "Hey," she said when she saw the handsome soldier standing on her porch.

Her mom backed out of the driveway without a wave, without even looking at Alice. She'd said she was proud of Alice and hoped she could build the family she wanted. But she wasn't exactly acting like it.

"Hey," he said, drawing Alice away from her thoughts about her mom. "I was worried I woke you up."

"Not at all," she said, stepping back. "You want to come in?"

He didn't move. "I hope it's okay that Clara came with." He indicated the dog. "You don't have cats or anything?"

"Cats?" She shook her head, a flirty smile planting itself on her face. "Hunter Magleby. Have you forgotten so much about me?"

"I remember everything about you," he said softly, his eyes dropping to his shoes for a moment. "I was hoping we could walk along the beach, and Clara loves to run. I don't get out with her as much as she needs, so I brought her."

More shock flowed through Alice. "The beach?" She'd actually avoided the beach as much as possible over the past ten years. The stretch of pristine sand at the bottom of the bluffs, directly below the Magleby Mansion, held precious memories for her.

She'd first kissed Hunter there. She'd married Hunter there. Everything about the beach screamed of Hunter, and she only went when she absolutely couldn't avoid it.

"All my memories of sand are bad now," he said. "So hot. No water. I want to remember what a good beach is like." He smiled at her, the movement gentle and yet revealing an edge of heat in his eyes that Alice had certainly seen before.

"Can you walk in the sand?" she asked.

"I'll be okay," he said.

"I'm glad I didn't put on a dress and heels." She gave him a coy smile and added, "Let me get my keys."

"I knew you wouldn't dress up," he said with a chuckle. "Not really your style, is it?"

"Are you calling me frumpy?" she called over her shoulder as she grabbed a jacket from the closet and her purse from the kitchen counter.

"I believe I used the word beautiful this morning."

Alice joined him on the porch, pulling the front door closed behind her. "Yeah, I guess you did."

Hunter took her hand in his, his grip firm enough to

make her pause and wait. He looked into her eyes, his expression intense and sincere. "I really like you, Alice Kopp."

Her mind flew back a dozen years, to when he'd said words like that before. Exactly like that, in fact.

"Hunter," she said, unsure of what else to add. She almost didn't dare hope that it had only taken him two weeks to forgive her. "Aren't you terribly angry with me?"

"I was," he said. "But the fury fades pretty fast, honestly." He gestured down to his injured right leg. "Same with this. I was so mad that I felt like I'd never *not* be mad about getting hurt."

He finally stepped, and she went with him. "But it went away. Then you go through other things. Denial. Hope. Sadness. Acceptance."

"Where are you right now?" she asked.

"With the leg? I think denial, as I think I'm going to be able to walk through sand." He grinned at her, pausing at the top of the steps. She only had five leading down, and she tried to imagine how she'd feel if she was him. Did five steps seem like a mountain?

Hunter was so strong, and so capable. Once, she'd believed he'd be able to protect her from anything. That as long as she had him, she could conquer mountains. As she moved slowly with him down the steps, she realized he was that same man. Still commanding the attention and respect of everyone around him. Still perfectly capable of taking care of himself—and her. And Westin.

They reached the bottom of the steps, and he said, "You know, last time I told you I liked you, you told me the same thing."

She giggled and went to tuck her hair behind her ear, but it was already up in that messy bun. "Yeah? You think you can remember that?"

"Oh, I remember it."

She branched away from him to go to the driver's side of the car while he went to the passenger. "I like you too, Hunter." She ducked her head and got in the car quickly. It screeched as she started it up, and Hunter frowned.

"I'm coming over to look at this car," he said. "On Saturday. Are you working then?"

"Tuesday, Thursday, Friday, Saturday," she recited like a robot. "Twelve hours each this week. Again." She rotated between the forty-eight-hour weeks and the forty-hour weeks, and she normally didn't mind the longer hours. "I hope the attending this week isn't Doctor Scoville."

"Jeremy Scoville?" Hunter asked.

"The one and the same."

"Is he still as arrogant?"

"Worse," Alice said with a groan. "You'd think he was a Magleby the way he struts around the hospital."

"Hey," Hunter protested. "Some of the Magleby's are great. Oh, by the way, I told my aunt we'd stop by on our way back from the beach. Apparently she has something for you."

"Your aunt Mabel has something for me?"

"That's what she said."

It was Alice's turn to frown. "I can't imagine what that would be."

"Well, I couldn't tell her no. I don't think anyone tells Mabel Magleby no." He smiled and shook his head. "And you're not getting away from me looking at this car." He held his hand in front of the heater vent. "This is barely blowing warm air."

"It takes a minute to warm up," she said, feeling defensive of her sedan. They'd been through a lot together, and she vividly remembered being able to purchase a vehicle of her own. "And it doesn't blow warm when it's stopped."

"Alice, you need a new car."

"I can't afford a new car," she said, cutting him a glance. "Buying this one was a major achievement. I was so proud of myself when I bought this eight-year-old used car." She laughed, but she wasn't ashamed of the memory. It was a good memory, one that had given her confidence and independence in a way she'd never had before.

For a moment, she thought Hunter might argue, but he didn't. He brooded as he looked out the windshield as she first went past his road and up the bluff to the Mansion. Then back down the other side, and around so they were back underneath it. She pulled off into the small parking lot, the car pointed toward the ocean they both loved.

"You were in a desert," she said. "All sand. No water."

"For a time."

"It was bad?"

"Very bad. The smell…you can't even imagine it."

"How long were you there?"

"Eight months." His voice suggested he didn't want to talk about it, so Alice searched her mind for another topic.

"Looks windy," she said, wanting to dig a hole and crawl into it for bringing up the weather.

"Wind I can deal with." He reached for the door handle and got out of the car. Alice joined him, shrugging into her jacket and flipping up the collar to keep the cold breeze from snaking down to more sensitive areas.

Hunter stood at the front of the car, one hand tucked into his pocket and the other gloved and resting on his cane. "I may have lied. This is wicked."

"Let's just go a little ways," she said. "Clara is already having fun." The golden retriever ran circles in the sand, kicking up clumps and trying to bite them. She barked every so often, and Alice giggled at her.

"Westin's always wanted a dog," she said.

"He told me," Hunter said.

"I'm so glad you two are getting along," Alice said, and she genuinely meant it.

"Me too," Hunter said. "Am I a bad person if I say I was worried he wouldn't like me?"

Alice laced her arm through his and they stepped out onto the sand. It was quite loose at first, but it quickly hardened. "No," she said, her own truth about to come out. "I'm worried he'll like you more than me, now that you're back and he's getting to know you."

"Oh, sweetheart, that's impossible."

"How do you know?" she asked.

"Because you're his mother. Children have a special bond with their mothers."

"Have you talked to yours since you've been back?" she asked.

His arm next to hers tightened, all the answer she needed. "Why not?" she asked.

"They don't live here anymore," he said. "I don't want her to feel bad that I chose to come here instead of San Diego." He sighed and surveyed the ocean, which foamed with whitecaps from the wicked wind. "Although, now that I'm thinking about it, I think I made the wrong choice."

Alice smiled at the gray sky, knowing how it felt to second-guess. "I don't think so, Hunter. I think you're right where you need to be."

"I meant about my mother." He whistled to Clara, whose head popped right up. She seemed to realize how far away she'd run, and she beelined back to them. "I got that job at Michaels Construction. I start tomorrow."

"Hunter," she said with brightness in her tone. "And you're just now telling me?" She nudged him, causing him to stumble a little worse than normal. "Oh, sorry." She gripped his arm tighter, pulling him into her. "Sorry."

He stopped, taking a moment to find a good spot for his cane. He looked at her. "I'm fine, Alice."

"I can see that," she murmured, her eyes dropping to his mouth. He wore a trim beard, something he'd grown over the past couple of weeks, and she wondered what it would feel like against her face.

Never one to mince words or talk things to death, Hunter leaned down and brushed his lips against hers. Hesitant and seeking, but absolutely in charge too. The wind went out as the flame between them roared to life.

Alice reached up with both hands and cradled his face, his beard soft against her skin. When she kissed him again, it held no reluctance, no surprise, and no regrets.

Kissing Alice on the beach was exquisite, just as it always had been. He'd be lying if he ever said he'd come to the beach thinking they'd just walk and talk. He'd been hoping with everything in him that he could find a moment that was just right to kiss her, and it had come.

She tasted like mint, and he knew she had barely woken in time to get ready to meet him. He wanted to feel guilty, and a single thread slipped through him. But mostly, he enjoyed the sparks popping in his bloodstream and the way she'd always fit so well in his arms, the shape of her lips seemingly made to kiss only him.

He pulled away first, long before he wanted to be done kissing her, and tucked her against his chest. The wind pounded against his back as Clara streaked in a circle around them. He laughed at the dog and said, "I brought a ball for her."

Throwing a ball for his dog required him to detangled himself from Alice and pluck the object from his pocket.

He launched it down the beach, watching as Clara streaked after it. Alice said, "Wow, look at her go," and Hunter turned back to her.

"I didn't get my picture today," he said.

Alice's beautiful, dark eyes shone at him in the waning light. "You'll get your picture, Mister. You're so impatient."

"It's been all day," he said, his stomach growling. He grinned at her. "And I'm hungry. You want to drive over to Bell Hill for something to eat?"

"Sure." She faced the ocean again. "I do love this beach."

"So you're not mad I lured you down here to kiss you?"

Their eyes met again, and Alice tipped her head back and laughed, revealing that slender, sexy neck. Hunter stared at it for a moment, and then switched his gaze to the water lapping at the shore too. Clara arrived with the ball and dropped it at his feet, eager for him to throw it again.

He couldn't help the groan that tore through his throat when he bent to pick up the ball. He threw it again, not nearly as far, and the dog took off again, spraying sand behind her.

"I'll bring you to the beach every day, if you want,"

Alice said, her way of saying she didn't mind him luring her to the beach for a kiss.

"Well, I have that job now," he said. "We might have to improvise with the locations."

Alice giggled, one of the most magical sounds to Hunter's ears. "You think you're so funny."

"I do not," he said. "If there's one thing I know I'm not, it's funny." He looked at her, dipping his head to kiss her again. He couldn't believe he'd been able to do this so easily. Well, there hadn't been much that had been easy about returning to Hawthorne Harbor and finding out he had a son.

But he really wasn't angry anymore. Worry gnawed at him a lot. Sometimes the sadness hit. He knew he wasn't finished grieving for his leg, nor the lost years with Westin. But he also knew that the more he interacted with Alice and Westin—and Karen—the more he liked them. He loved his son, and the old, rusted over feelings he had for Alice were starting to bloom again too.

So he'd do the same thing with his relationship that he was doing with his physical therapy. Take one step at a time.

HUNTER SAT IN FRONT OF THE COMPUTER THE NEXT morning, his brain already on overload. Lauren had shown him about four hundred things before she'd breezed out the door with, "I'm at the Phillips job site this morning, and I'll be at the Mansion this afternoon."

He'd nodded and lifted his hand in a farewell wave she hadn't seen. And now he was trying to figure out what to do with the stack of papers and folders she had on the desk. These needed to be recorded and filed, but he couldn't remember what program she'd said to use for that.

His mind lingered on Alice anyway. They'd gone to Bell Hill to a hole-in-the-wall diner that he'd loved growing up. Then they'd spent an hour with Mabel at her cottage on the hill. Flashbacks of falling had hit him for a moment, and he hadn't wandered off on his own.

Clara, dirty but happy, had slept at his feet while Mabel gave Alice a book of remembrances from their wedding a decade ago.

Hunter's chest still pinched thinking about it. Why hadn't his great aunt given this to her years ago? Why had she kept it until now? Hunter hadn't known what to say or do, so he'd let the two women gush over the flowers and the food from their marriage so long ago.

A marriage than Alice had then gotten legally annulled. Cancelled, as if it had never happened. Void, as if their union, their honeymoon, their life—short as it was —together had been a piece of garbage she just wanted to throw away.

Hunter struggled through the evening with his anger,

wishing he'd moved all the way past it but knowing he hadn't. Even with the kissing he and Alice had done.

He felt better this morning, and he exhaled as he picked up the piece of paper on the top of the pile. It was an invoice that had been mailed, and Hunter placed it in a clear spot on the desk.

Piece by piece, pile by pile, he sorted the folders, files, and papers until he had them grouped into reasonable things.

Upon opening the desk drawer, he found files and put all the stacks into the right folders. He'd start organizing things on the computer from this moment forward, but he wasn't going to go back and try to make sense of a system that didn't exist.

His stomach growled, and he realized he'd spent hours going through the things Lauren had been tossing in piles. Her offices sat in a tiny rental space around the corner from the Anchor, and Hunter hadn't been back to Main Street since he'd returned to town.

Thinking now a better time than most, he put on his jacket and stood up. He'd been sitting for a long time, so his right leg tingled and twitched for a few seconds. He waited for the muscles to calm before trying to use them, and he braved the rainy day to go get some lunch.

The atmosphere in the Anchor was exactly what he expected and remembered. Loud. Vibrant. Laughter. Conversation. The scent of freshly baked bread and slow roasted meat met his nose, with the hint of bacon underneath that.

His mouth watered as he joined the line behind a pair of women chatting about their kids and their next family vacation.

Everything felt so normal, and for someone like Hunter who'd been removed from the everyday happenings of regular life, everything seemed foreign for a few moments.

Then his mind caught up with reality, and he felt for a moment that he did fit here, with the rest of humanity, in the line to get a sandwich from the best deli in the state of Washington.

He didn't like the crowd or the noise, but he clenched his teeth and focused on the menu board to job his memory of what he liked here. Ah, yes. The Small Yacht, minus the jalapeños. He definitely couldn't tolerate the spicy stuff since being blown up. His four surgeries had been on his leg, but they'd somehow affected his stomach and what he could eat.

He'd just stepped up to the cash register to order when he met the eyes of the woman standing there. "Welcome to the—Hunter Magleby?"

It was as if she'd bellowed into a megaphone. It seemed to go quiet around him, and Hunter glanced to the pair of women now on his left that had ordered ahead of him. They both watched him, and he looked back at the woman who should be taking his order.

"I'm sorry," he said as diplomatically as possible. "Do we know each other?"

"Yes," she said, smiling a big old fake smile. "I'm Karly Best. I was a bridesmaid at your wedding." Her eyes rounded, and she leaned forward. "Does Alice know you're back in town?"

"I've seen her," he said, the nonchalance in his voice sky high.

"So sad about what happened," she said, shaking her head.

Hunter just wanted to order his sandwich and go back to the quiet office. Sure, it was small, but no one pretended there. There wasn't anyone else there at all.

"What happened?" Hunter asked, curious to know what the rumors were around town. After all, he'd been gone for a long time. Did everyone know Westin was his son? Foolishness and bitterness became friends in his chest, and he regretted his question.

"You know, with Alice getting so sick and moving to Vancouver with her aunt." Karly really looked like she was sad about it, but Hunter had a hard time believing that.

"Her aunt actually lives in British Colombia," Hunter said. "I'll take the Small Yacht on white. No jalapeños, and can you have them throw on extra bacon?" He gazed evenly at Karly, who took an extra moment to tap in his order. He paid and stepped over to the throng of people waiting.

The two moms made room for him, and one of them

touched his arm. "Thanks for your service, Hunter." She seemed nothing but genuine, and pride filled his chest. He tamped it down, for he was just doing his job.

"Thank you," he said. "I don't think I know you either."

She smiled, but it was completely different from Karly's fake grin. "No, you don't. I'm Terri Thompson. Your mother was my Sunday School teacher when you were a little boy. I really loved her. It was sad when your parents left town."

That familiar sadness welled in his gut, and he nodded. "Thank you. I'll tell her." And that meant he'd have to finally call her. It was time anyway, but Hunter still hadn't quite found the right words to say. There were no right words.

He loved his parents, and they loved him. They'd supported his decision to marry Alice and enlist in the Marines. He wasn't exactly sure what had happened that had prompted them to leave Hawthorne Harbor, but if he spent many more afternoons with Aunt Mabel, he was sure he could figure it out.

The very idea of trying to hunt down gossip made him tired. He just wanted his sandwich and his dog and a nap.

On and whim, he pulled out his phone and found Alice's text string. I know you're not working today. What are the chances you could pick me up in town and take me home?

Lauren would understand. She'd said Hunter could take things slowly. And he'd already cleaned off her whole desk. Now, he just wanted to eat and take a nap with Clara curled up at his feet.

His phone buzzed. I can do that. Where are you?

And Alice, he thought. He wanted to eat. He wanted to rest. And he wanted to kiss Alice until he felt like she'd never toss him aside again.

14

Alice found Hunter on the curb, right at the address where he'd said he'd be. He came around the front of her car, frowning at the hood, and handed her a bag through the window with the words, "Can you hold this for a sec?"

She took it, the scent of freshly baked bread and roast beef making her mouth water. This lunch would be so much better than what she normally ate.

Hunter slid into the passenger seat, his expression completely unreadable. She passed the food back to him after he buckled in, and she asked, "Your place?"

"Yes, please," he said, his voice on the deathly edge of quiet.

Alice drove, humming to herself to the song on the radio. With every turn and every minute that passed, the tension in the car dropped.

"Want to tell me what happened?" she asked when she pulled up to his cabin on Forgotten Road.

"I ran into one of your bridesmaids from our wedding," he said. "She said it was

'so sad' about you getting sick and going to live with your aunt." He turned toward her, a look of agony in his eyes.

"People talk in a small town," she said. "I needed a buffer and some time." She'd done a lot of things wrong but getting out of Hawthorne Harbor to have Westin and make some decisions wasn't one of them.

"I know," he said. "I just...it kind of put me over the edge." The bag crinkled in his fingers as he gripped it tighter and reached for the door handle. As he twisted, she caught sight of a scar extending up from beneath his coat collar.

His injury wasn't just in his leg, and a flash of sorrow for him hit her hard. She got out of the car and joined him in going up the steps and into the house. They sat at the table, and he pulled out the sandwiches.

"You got me the Beach Club?" she asked.

"It's your favorite," he said, looking at her. "Has those avocadoes you love." A smite twitched against his lips, and Alice grinned outright.

"Thank you, Hunter." She wasn't sure why such a small gesture meant so much to her. She leaned over and kissed him, the moment turning from sweet to heated quite quickly. He curled his fingers in her hair and deepened their kiss until Alice was light-headed—and not from the way her stomach screamed at her for food.

He pulled away and cleared his throat, and when Alice opened her eyes, she found a ruddy flush in his face. She felt that same heat radiating through her whole body, and she picked up her sandwich to unwrap it.

"Tell me something about you I've forgotten," he said.

"I thought you said you remembered everything about me," she teased.

"Surely you have something new in the last nine years." He lifted his sandwich to his lips.

"I don't mind mowing the lawn," she said.

Hunter chuckled as he peeled the paper off his sandwich and lifted the top of it. A flicker of displeasure ran through his eyes. There, then gone. He proceeded to peel a few slices of jalapeno off his sandwich as he said, "I know you were worried about that before we got married. Had never mowed the lawn."

"I do it all the time now," she said, as if she deserved a medal for completing such a simple chore.

"That's great. You can come do mine."

"I'm sure Westin could do it," she said, wondering if she really wanted her to mow his lawn. She didn't think so. Not the strong, proud Hunter Magleby. He'd hire a service before he let her come help him, she was sure of that.

"Oh, that's a great idea," he said. "I'll teach him once it warms up."

"Great, then he can do our too."

Hunter cocked his head at her and lifted his sandwich to his lips. She wasn't sure what she'd said wrong, and he simply kept eating. When he finished, he groaned as he stood and moved into the living room.

"Come on, girl," he said to Clara, patting the couch beside him. The dog jumped up and curled into his left side, and he sighed.

"Thanks for lunch," Alice said, crumpling up both of their wrappers and throwing them in the garbage.

"You're going?"

"You look like you're going to take a nap." She smiled at him to soften the words. "Which is fine. I have to get Westin from school in a couple of hours anyway."

"Stay until then," he said, looking at her with those intense eyes of his. "And maybe I'll go with you to get him."

Alice wasn't sure what to make of that, so she just nodded.

Hunter patted the couch on the other side of him. "You can sit right here, sweetheart."

"Oh, so you're going to flirt with me and *then* fall asleep."

"I might stay awake," he said.

She giggled as she walked in front of him, careful not to touch his injured leg, and sat beside him. He took her hand in his, another sigh seeping from his mouth. "Yeah, I like this."

Alice took a moment to bask in the situation. She rarely just sat around in the middle of the day, but today, she experienced a sense of peace. Being in Hunter's cabin felt wonderful, and right, and the way his hand fit in hers made it seem like they'd been constructed that way and then separated later.

Her eyes drifted closed too, and an image of what her life could be like if they were a real family swam behind her eyelids. She'd only woken up next to Hunter three times, and yet, she could still see it so clearly. Feel the warmth of him beside her.

"How bad is your leg?" she asked, her voice barely more than a whisper.

"Bad," he whispered back.

"Are you in pain all the time?"

"When I'm not moving, I'm okay," he said. "Sleeping is okay, but sometimes I worry so much that I'll do something to it, that I don't sleep very soundly."

"I'm so sorry," she said. "I saw a scar on your neck too."

"Yeah, that's from a piece of debris," he said. "I have some burn scars down that right side too, along my back."

"Do they hurt?"

"No."

"How long has it been since you got hurt?"

"Six months," he said. "I had to have four surgeries, and they didn't release me until the doctors were sure they'd done all they could."

Alice's whole soul ached for him. She didn't want to

pity him or say she was sorry again. They were nice words, but they didn't do anything. She squeezed his fingers. "Can I lean into you on this side?"

"Try it, and we'll see," he said.

Carefully, gingerly, not wanting to cause him any more suffering, she laid her head against his bicep. She was instantly transported back to the first time they'd ridden the Ferris wheel together. He'd held her hand, just like she was now. She'd leaned into him, just like she was now.

She'd been in love with him, just like she was now.

"That's just fine, sweetheart," he murmured, touching his lips to her forehead. His breath cascaded over her face before he turned, and Alice emitted her own happy little sigh to be there with him as she was now.

A couple of hours later, she went down the front steps and said, "Will the car still start? It's time to go get Westin."

Hunter straightened from where he'd been bent over looking at the engine. "Yeah, it'll start. You need a new timing belt. Some spark plugs, and your power steering system needs to be flushed and refilled."

That all sounded expensive. Why did cars have to have belts? Alice was sure they weren't the kind that held up pants and couldn't be bought in the department store on Main Street. "I haven't noticed a problem with the power steering."

"Does your car squeal?"

"It has in the past."

"I'll get everything you need and get it fixed up." He smiled at her, took an extra moment to balance himself, and reached both hands up to put the hood down. "You're driving." He flipped the keys in her direction, and she managed to catch them before they impaled her in the face. "And can we stop for ice cream on the way home?"

She shook her head and laughed as she got in the car.

"No?" he asked when he joined her. "We can't have ice cream?"

"I'm sure we can have ice cream," she said.

"Good," Hunter said, settling in. Alice liked this easiness between them, and she sent up a quick pleading to anyone listening that he would be able to forgive her and that this day could somehow become her reality.

"You seem upset," Alice said to her mother a week later. "You barely look at me when I bring Westin over. Hunter says you don't really talk to him." Her mother continued to fly around the kitchen as if she were a Tasmanian devil. She was making a chocolate pie for the bake-off fundraiser at the community center, and Alice had made the mousse a few times herself.

There were a lot of little steps, using three different kitchen utensils, but still. Her mother had talked her way through an entire strawberry shortcake one time, so she could definitely spare a few brain cells for speaking.

"I'm not upset," she said again. "I'm adjusting."

Alice nodded, her lips pressed together as she watched her mother lift a ladle of hot cream into the eggs. She whisked furiously, adding, "And I like that I have more time to do my own thing. And spend time with your dad. I do. But sometimes...." She let her words hang there while she poured the now tempered eggs into the cream and switched from a wooden spoon to a whisk to keep the custard from burning.

"Sometimes," Alice prompted.

"Sometimes I catch myself thinking, 'Oh, it's time to go get Westin,' or 'Maybe Westin would like chicken nuggets for dinner.' And then I remember I don't need to do any of that." She kept her eyes trained down into the pot.

"I know, Mom." She'd been going through a lot of adjustments herself. Spending time alone was new for her, and she needed to figure out a balance between doing nothing and filling her life with meaningful hobbies.

Hunter did not bother her during the day, and she appreciated that he respected her sleeping schedule. She couldn't help thinking through what their life would be like should they see this relationship all the way through to the end again.

Her mother would likely have to still come get Westin and take him to school. Or maybe Trent or Lauren could do it. Alice rarely got off in time to get her son where he needed to go.

Then she'd come home to the cabin, and she'd been

dreaming of kissing him before he went to work and she went to bed. Holding onto those broad shoulders and smiling up at him like she'd done before.

Her mother moved the pot off the burner, bringing Alice back to the present with the words, "Add that butter in here, Alice."

She dropped the chopped butter into the pot and her mother switched to a rubber spatula. "I'm sorry about all the changes, Mom."

"I'm not," she said. "Not even for a moment. But it's hard. I know it's the right thing. Doesn't mean it's easy or instant. I'm working on it."

"I guess that's the best any of us can do."

"Hunter is...." She cleared her throat and paused in her rapid folding to get the butter melted. She scooped up a handful of the melted chocolate and put it in the pot. After using the knife to get it all off the chopping block, she went back to stirring, this time to melt the chocolate and complete the custard.

"Hunter is a very good man," she said. "He's a great father." She stepped over to the prepared crust and poured the custard into it.

"Is he?" Alice asked. "What makes you say that?"

"I've seen him with Westin. He's got a job now, and he's fixing your car, and he's basically doing everything you always told me he would." She faced Alice and wiped her bangs out of her eyes with the back of her wrist. "Right, Alice? Didn't you tell me for weeks that he was good, that he'd take care of you, that you loved him?"

Alice had, yes. She nodded, her emotions too tight in the back of her throat. Her mother washed her hands and reached for the plastic wrap. As she patted it onto the top of the hot custard so it wouldn't form a skin as it cooled, she said, "Well, I'm finally seeing it in him. It's good, like I said. I'm just adjusting."

"Fair enough," Alice said. "It has been a big adjustment for everyone." She glanced at the clock. "I'm going to be late." She stepped over to her mom and gave her a side-hug. "I love you, Mom."

"I love you too, Alice. Have a good session."

Alice grabbed her purse and headed for the door, only checking quickly to watch Westin throw a basketball toward the hoop after she'd pulled out of the driveway. She hadn't told Hunter she was in counseling yet, and her mom needed a few extra hours with Westin.

As Alice drove away, she decided there was no better time than to call him and tell him right now. So she did.

15

As January faded into February, the town of Hawthorne Harbor grew in excitement for the Spring Fling. Hunter had never really cared much for it, though he welcomed back the warmer weather and apple blossoms as much as anyone else.

He woke one morning in February with guilt on his conscience, and he knew it was because he hadn't yet told his mother about Westin. He wasn't sure why making the phone call was so hard, and he had sudden appreciation for what Alice had been through in the past.

He got Westin ready for school and down the steps before Karen arrived. She got out of the car, as she'd been doing every day since they'd been late on the second day. "Morning, boys," she said with a smile. "Got everything, Westie? Lunch and all that?"

"It's mashed potato day," he and Hunter said together, and Karen burst out laughing.

"You two are like clones," she said. "If I hadn't been there when this little one was born, I'd wonder if he was really my daughter's." She beamed at Westin, but a strange sense of jealousy moved through Hunter.

Of course Alice's mother would've been at the birth. Just because she'd moved away from Hathorne Harbor didn't mean she'd cut her family out of her life.

"Oh, it was nothing," Karen said, putting her hand on Hunter's arm. He looked at it and then her.

"What was nothing?"

"The birth," she said. "You didn't miss much."

"You think I didn't miss much when I missed the birth of my son?"

"Of course not," she said, sighing. "That's not what I meant." Her fingers tightened on his arm. "I'm so sorry, Hunter. Had I known she hadn't told you, I would've. A man should know when he has a child."

Hunter's emotions morphed from angry and frothing to soft in a second. "Thank you, Karen. That means a lot coming from you."

"You're so good with him," she said, glancing at Westin in the car, watching them. "Better than Alice sometimes."

"That's not true," Hunter said, jumping to her defense. "Moms are just different."

Karen looked at him again, appreciation in her eyes. "That's true."

"We're still good for this afternoon?" he asked, his pride shriveling a bit.

"Yes," she said. "I'll be back at one." With that, she got in the car and rumbled off to take Westin to school. And later, she'd return to take him to his physical therapy appointment and then the automotive store, where Alice's fuel pump and timing belt had finally come in. He'd get the car finished that afternoon, and she should continue to run for a while.

He returned to the house, telling Clara to "Close it," so he could focus on his phone—and the call he needed to make to his mother.

Her line rang and rang, and she finally picked up with a breathless, "Hello?"

"Mom," he said, his voice catching on the three-letter word. "It's Hunter."

"Hunter." She sucked in a breath. "Is it really you? Westin, it's Hunter." The excitement and emotion in her voice only made Hunter feel worse.

"It's really me, Mom."

"Hunter?" his dad said, his voice echoing through the line. "We put you on speaker."

Hunter pressed his eyes closed and took a deep, deep breath, his son's name mirroring his father's. "Hey, Dad."

"Where are you?" his mother asked. "Do you need us to come pick you up?"

How could he tell her he'd been back in Hawthorne Harbor for weeks? *Just do it*, he told himself. "Just a sec," he said. "I need to sit down." He limped over to the couch and sat right in the middle of it, imagining Betsy on his right the way she'd been a couple of weeks ago.

"I'm so excited to hear your voice," his mother said. "I can't believe it."

"Let him talk, Darlene," his father said, his voice muted.

"I have a lot to tell you," Hunter said. "It's...not all good. So which do you want first? The good news or the bad news?"

"Bad," his mother said.

Hunter pulled in his breath and held it, gearing up to say what he deemed the worst news. "I'm permanently injured and have been honorably discharged from the Marines."

"Permanently injured?" His mother's voice pitched up.

"But the good news to that is I'm still alive, and I have both legs."

"Hunter," his mother said, but he kept going. She liked to interject, and it felt cleansing to him to say this out loud. Acknowledge it, the way he did other things. Like he had with his feelings for Alice.

"Semi-good news is I'm living for free and have a great retirement and health benefits."

"Why is that semi-good news?" his mom asked.

"I'm in Hawthorne Harbor," he said, waiting for the bomb to drop.

"Oh," she said, "I...wasn't expecting that."

"Lauren lives right down the road, and Aunt Mabel has been nothing but wonderful."

"Yes, well, it never was her that disapproved of us so much," his mom said.

"Darlene," his dad said again. "Hunter, we'd love to come visit."

"I'm sure you would," he said. "Especially after I tell you this next thing." Neither of his parents said anything, and yet Hunter couldn't order the words. His mind flashed through a series of scenes, each with Westin one step closer to him in the hospital atrium, and Alice saying, *He's your son, Hunter.*

"I'm sure you remember Alice Kopp," he started. "Well, turns out we had...she had a baby. My baby. A son. I have a son."

Silence poured through the line, but Hunter didn't know how to fill it.

"How long have you been back in Hawthorne Harbor?" his dad finally asked, and Hunter's mind clicked around.

"The boy is almost nine," he said. "He's from when we were married before. She never told me, and I just found out when I returned to town, about a month ago." It was a week or two longer than a month, but he didn't want to hurt his parents more than necessary.

"Westin, we are going right now," his mother said. "Let's fly."

"Hunter," his dad said, a clear plea for more information.

He stroked Clara's head beside him on the couch. "She named him Westin, Dad. He looks just like us. He's smart, and wonderful, and I can't wait for you to meet him."

"Westin?" his mother asked in a haunted whisper, and Hunter heard sniffling through the line.

"Come whenever," he said, barely holding back his own emotions. "I can't come get you at the airport, but Aunt Mabel will send her driver. Or there are dozens of other Magleby's who'll come, I'm sure."

"Anytime?" his mom asked. "You don't have a job?"

"I do, but it's flexible," he said. "I take care of Westin in the evenings, and Alice's mother takes him to school in the morning. Alice is a urse on the graveyard shift."

"Just like me," his mom said.

"You'll need to get time off," his dad said. "We can't just leave today."

"No, you're right." His mother sighed. "Hunter, we're going to come. I just need to work out a few things with my job."

"Anytime," Hunter said. "I can send you some pictures." He realized he should've been forwarding Alice's Picture of the Day to them all this time.

"We would love that," his dad said. "We'll talk to you soon."

"Love you guys," Hunter said.

"We love you too," they chorused together, and the call

ended. He let his hand drop to his lap and leaned his head against the back of the couch. He wasn't sure why that phone call had been so hard, only that it was.

He also knew that his parents would come to Hawthorne Harbor as soon as they could, and it would cost them more than the price of a plane ticket. He wondered if his mother had spoken to hers recently, and he concluded that she probably hadn't.

It didn't matter. His grandmother surely knew he was back in town too, and he hadn't even seen her or spoken to her. It was definitely not Aunt Mabel his parents needed to prep to see, and Hunter felt bad for coming back to this town when he'd had his choice of anywhere in the world.

Then he thought of Westin and Alice, and he knew somehow, by some power, he'd been led right where he was supposed to be.

"It can't be mashed potato day again," Hunter said, the brown paper sack in his hand already open. "You had that yesterday."

"It's chicken bowl day," Westin said, tipping the tablet toward Hunter. "See? It's mashed potatoes, then all these chicken bites. It has corn and then all this gravy. It's *soo* good."

Hunter chuckled and said, "All right," putting the bag

back in the drawer. "But if you want really good mashed potatoes, we should go down to Forks to the Spud Shop there. There's nothing like them."

"Yeah?" Westin asked. "When can we go?"

Hunter's mind buzzed, and he hated that his body couldn't be as active. "Well, I can't drive, bud. We'll have to talk to your mom."

Westin pouted. "Dang. I wanted to go today."

Hunter scoffed, sure his son was kidding. "You have school today."

"So?" he asked. "We don't do anything."

"You don't do anything at school?" Hunter shook his head and picked up Westin's empty cereal bowl. "I find that hard to believe."

"It's true," Westin said. "And we're having a sub anyway, because Miss Riley is out of town for her daughter's baby."

So they really wouldn't be doing anything.... Hunter picked up his phone. "Let me call Aunt Mabel. Maybe Jaime can take us."

"Are you serious?" Westin jumped up from the table and whooped before dancing around. Clara got up, startled, and watched him run around the table with apprehension on her face.

"Slow down," Hunter said with a laugh as his great aunt's line rang.

She finally picked up with a "What can I do for you this morning, Hunter?"

"I'm wondering how busy Jaime is," he started. "Westin and I would like to go to the Spud Shop for some mashed potatoes. You're invited, of course."

"Mashed potatoes?" she practically barked. "Why would I need to drive for two hours for mashed potatoes?"

"Because they're the best ones in the state," Hunter said matter-of-factly. "And we love mashed potatoes." He laughed as Westin's eyes widened and he nodded so energetically it looked like his head would come off.

"Pish posh," Aunt Mabel said. "But I'll ask Jaime."

"Thank you," Hunter said. He hung up and looked at Westin. "She has to ask Jaime."

"So we don't know?"

"Not yet, bud." For some reason, Hunter really wanted to give him whatever he wanted, even if it cost him a day of school. Lauren would understand. In fact, she probably wouldn't even know if he skipped organizing a filing cabinet she hadn't opened in five years.

A text came in that said, *Jaime will be there at ten*, and Hunter promptly said, "We're gold. I better call your grandma. I hope she hasn't left yet." Her pick-up time was twenty minutes away still, but Karen was nothing if not prompt and punctual.

"We're gold," Westin repeated, and Hunter grinned as Alice's mother answered the phone.

"Karen," he said. "I hope you haven't left yet. Westin won't be needing a ride to school today...."

"He did?" Alice looked at her phone again, sure the text message from the school about Westin missing that day was wrong. Westin never missed school, unless he was deathly ill. And if he was deathly ill, Hunter should've called her.

She dialed him, frustrated when his line rang and rang and then went to voicemail. "Hunter, did you know Westin missed school today? Call me back, please."

She decided to try her mother, worrying needling her heart and her stomach simultaneously in the most unpleasant way. Her mom picked up, and Alice said, "Did you know Westin missed school today?"

"Yes," she said, utterly nonplussed. "He and Hunter went to Forks."

"Forks? What in the world?" Alice couldn't think of

anything else to say. Why would Hunter take Westin to forks on a Thursday? It made no sense.

"Something about mashed potatoes," she said as the doorbell chimed in the background. "I have to run, dear. The plumber's here."

Alice stared at her phone after the call ended, trying to decide how she felt. Confused, sure. Frustrated, definitely.

And angry.

She was angry Hunter had allowed their son to miss school over something frivolous like mashed potatoes. Not only that, but he hadn't even *asked* her. There'd been no text. Was he even going to tell her she didn't need to wake up and drive over to the elementary school and wait in that pick-up line?

She shook her phone like it was a magic eight-ball and could give her the answers to her questions. Of course it didn't. It did, however, show her a partial reflection of her face, and wow, she did not look happy.

"I'm not happy," she muttered to herself as she got up and padded into the bathroom. At the risk of coming across the wrong way, she called Hunter again. He still didn't pick up, and she didn't bother to leave a message.

He wouldn't listen to it anyway. She texted him instead, with, I heard you took Westin to Forks today. It would have been nice to know I didn't need to set my alarm and get up to go pick him up at the elementary school.

She knew she shouldn't text when she was angry, but she sent the message anyway. She had a right to be angry.

After last night's busy shift—her third in a row—she'd been exhausted, and she could've slept for another couple of hours at least.

Her phone stayed dark and silent, even when she stared at it with her most potent Mom-glare. She wanted to throw it against the wall and then drive over to Hunter's cabin. Instead, she set it on silent and got into the shower.

That only worked for about one minute, and then she craned her neck to see if there was a blue light flashing along the top of the device. She couldn't see through the steam and water spraying against the glass.

So she had a completely unfulfilling shower, almost drowning her phone as she stepped out of the stall. Still no text.

As calmly as she could, she got dressed and threw her hair up into a messy topknot that would probably drip water for at least an hour. Didn't matter. She needed to get over to Hunter's so he'd know she wasn't pleased with his choices that day.

She drove slowly, reminding herself that Hunter was a grown man. He wasn't her child, and while she had the right to be upset, she wouldn't lecture him. Or nag him. Or any of those things she wanted to do—which she naturally did with Westin.

Her phone buzzed as she merged onto the highway that would lead her up to the bluff.

Hey, Mom. Sorry we didn't text you. Dad just said we should just now. We're on our way back.

Some of the fight left her body, but she continued on to Hunter's place. She parked and kept the heater blowing while she waited. And waited. With each passing minute, more of her anger lessened, but her impatience grew.

She'd been camped in front of his cabin for an hour before the long luxury car pulled up and Westin and Hunter and Clara spilled out.

They all wore smiles—even the dog—and the two humans waved to Jaime. He positively beamed back at them before driving down to the end of the lane to turn around.

Alice unfolded herself from her sedan, which ran pretty good now that Hunter had been under the hood of it.

"Mom," Westin said in a chipper voice, running over to her. "You would not believe what I did today."

"No," she said dryly, catching Hunter's eye as he moved closer too. "I'm sure I wouldn't."

"We went on a road trip!" Westin punched the air like he'd just won a gold medal. "And all we ate today was potatoes. Well, that's not really true. I had cereal for breakfast, but that doesn't count because we decided to go on the road trip after breakfast." He kept chattering away, his voice becoming distant in Alice's mind as Hunter arrived and pressed a kiss to her cheek.

"You coming in?" he asked, continuing on past her toward the steps.

"I don't think so," she said, her voice like ice.

Hunter paused and looked back, her displeasure with him finally registering in his eyes. "You go on, bud," he said to Westin. "Mom and I will come in just a sec."

Somehow, Westin didn't seem to mind that he was talking to Clara, and the two of them went inside, leaving Alice alone with Hunter in front of the house.

"He can't just skip school whenever he wants," she said.

"He didn't want to," Hunter said. "I suggested it, and he just went along with it."

"Fine." She folded her arms. "*You* can't just take him out of school whenever you want."

"Why not?" Hunter challenged. "He's eight years old. He's not trying to win a presidential scholarship."

"They actually give out a Hope of America award."

He scoffed and rolled his eyes. "Yeah, I know all about that. You know who wins crap like that? People like Jeremy Scoville." He gazed at her, anger sparking in those dark eyes. "It was one day. We had fun." He turned as if this conversation was over, and that annoyed Alice even further.

"I'm sorry I didn't text you so you didn't have to get up," he said over his shoulder. "That was a mistake I'll own." He started up the steps, and it looked painstakingly slow and awkward.

"Hunter," she said after him.

"Alice," he said in that quiet voice lined with danger.

"I'm exhausted and it's cold out here. If you want to keep lecturing me, please come inside."

"I am not lecturing you," she said. "I was trying very hard not to do that."

He said nothing, and she went up the few steps he had and then slowed to his pace. He paused just outside the front door and looked at her. "I'm his father. I knew where he was, and it was one day of school. Third grade. It doesn't even matter."

"I don't want him to think he can do that whenever he wants."

"He doesn't think that."

"And I know you're his father."

"Do you?" Hunter challenged. "Because I didn't realize I had to ask your permission to do things with our son." He reached to open the door, but Alice put her hand on his, stopping him.

"Of course I know you're his father," she said, heat running through her blood. "And I realize that we've never parented together." A storm swirled in her chest. "So we need to work on that."

Hunter looked like he had the same tornado attacking him. Quickly, much quicker than Alice's, it blew itself out. "Yes," he said. "You're right about that."

She nodded, opened the door, and went inside first, scooping Westin into her arms for a hug. "I'm glad you had a fun day with Dad."

"You're not mad?"

"She's mad," Hunter said.

"I am not," Alice argued.

He simply limped over to the couch and practically collapsed onto it with a loud groan. "Westie, can you get me a bottle of water from the fridge and the painkillers in the drawer beside it?"

"Yep." Westin wiggled out of her arms and skipped into the kitchen, seemingly unconcerned about his dad's health. Alice wasn't. She watched as Hunter downed four pills and then leaned his head back into the couch, his eyes drifting closed.

Clara jumped up beside him, and his arm naturally went around her, stroking her neck and side.

"Come on, Westin," she said. "Dad's really tired from your fun road trip. Let's let him rest."

"All right." Westin ran over to Hunter and hugged him. "Bye, Dad. See you later."

Hunter hugged him back and looked at Alice. "I'm sorry I didn't text."

"Thank you," she said.

"When you bring him back, can you bring dinner? I'll pay for it."

She nodded again, motioning for Westin to come. Half of her wanted to stay here with Hunter. Be a family. Let Westin watch something on TV or go down the road to Porter's house. She didn't want to leave and take him to a different house. He shouldn't be so divided.

But she wanted to talk to him alone too, and maybe

she needed a few more minutes to cool all the way down. So she turned and headed for the door, the exhaustion in Hunter's face making her heart wrench painfully in her chest.

"There they are," she said to Westin. He almost threw his chicken nugget as he whipped around to look at the entrance to the play place.

Alice had called in reinforcements in the form of fast food and other single moms. Karen Mullen carried the tray with food on it, and her little girl ran toward Westin and Alice.

"Hey, Cadence," Alice said.

"Hey."

"Can I go?" Westin asked.

He hadn't finished eating yet, but Karen didn't have rules for Cadence. And Alice was tired of thinking about whether she was doing something wrong or right with her son. She nodded and the two kids whooped and ran for the slides and jungle gym several feet away.

"Hey." Karen sighed as she slid her tray onto the table and sat down. "You okay? You never call in the middle of the day like this."

"It's almost dinnertime," Alice said, though it was barely four-thirty.

"Sure," Karen said, going along with it. She tucked her

honeyed hair behind her ear and looked at the slides before moving food around on the tray and then unwrapping her straw. "So what's going on?"

"Remember how I texted you that Hunter Magleby was back in town?"

"Yes." She plucked fries from the box and ate them.

"I don't know what to do about him."

"*Do* about him?" Karen looked at her with bright blue eyes.

"How do you and Glenn get along...I mean, make parenting decisions for Cadence?"

"Glenn doesn't see her enough to make parenting decisions."

"He sees her on weekends and in the summer. Surely he has to make some decisions." Alice just needed someone to throw her a life preserver. She felt adrift in a new sea of joint parenting she didn't understand and had never navigated.

"We didn't break up because we couldn't agree how to parent," Karen said. "Maybe if you just tell me what happened, I can help."

Alice sighed and dragged another fry she wouldn't eat through the pile of ketchup. "Okay." So she told the story, and Karen was the best friend in the whole world. She gasped and shook her head, and said, "He did not," in all the right places.

Alice felt better just talking to her, because she felt validated.

"Okay," Karen said. "So you talked to him. He apologized. You told Westin he can't ask his dad to take him on road trips all the time." She shrugged and grinned at Cadence as the little girl came back for a bite of her burger. As she skipped off again, still chewing—something Alice never would've allowed—Karen said, "Sounds like you handled it fine."

She nodded, but she didn't want to just "handle it." She didn't want to deal with it again.

"So you and Hunter," Karen said. "You two going to get back together?"

Hope jolted through Alice as if someone had hooked her up to a live wire. She caught the words before they left her mouth, and she changed them into, "Maybe. I don't know."

She'd been feeling all sorts of soft things for Hunter, and she did love him on some level. Even Karen had said she still loved Glenn. They just couldn't live together anymore. Was that Alice's same fate? Would she forever be driving her son to his father's house and then picking him up from school?

She wasn't sure, and that made her heart heavier than it had been in a very long time.

17

A week passed after the road trip, and Hunter felt a new band of tension between him and Alice. Sure, she brought dinner sometimes. She was punctual and polite when she brought Westin. But the fire that had burned between them so brightly had faded to a few coals.

She let him hold her hand once, and she kissed him good-bye in the evenings. But there was definitely something lurking beneath the surface and he had no idea when it would come splashing out.

He'd been sending pictures of him and Westin to his parents, along with all the pictures Alice had given him of Westin growing up.

We'll be there tomorrow about three, his mom's text read, and his heart pulsed out an extra beat. Of course he knew they'd love Westin. And Westin was so good at meeting and interacting with other people. When Hunter had asked him if he was nervous to meet a new set of grandparents, he'd said, "Not really."

"Why not?" Hunter had asked.

"I stay with people all the time," Westin said. "I'm sure they'll be nice." He'd looked at Hunter with a sliver of apprehension then. "They're nice, right?"

"Of course they are,"

Hunter had said. And they were. They'd left Hawthorne Harbor over a disagreement, but Hunter wasn't sure what it was. He knew the Magleby family wasn't perfect, even if a lot of them acted like they were. Yes, most of them had stayed in town, but there were several who'd left too.

Lauren didn't seem to take any flack for living here when her parents didn't, and Hunter was glad for it. No one bothered him either.

Sounds good, he said. *Jaime will bring us to the airport.* They were flying into Seattle, and Hunter had already cleared it with Alice for Westin to miss school so they could drive up and pick up his parents. They were staying in Seattle for the night, actually, and then they'd spend the weekend in Hawthorne Harbor.

His stomach vibrated just thinking about them returning to this town they didn't like, and he distracted himself by opening the accounts payable spreadsheet and entering in some receipts Lauren had left on the desk.

The office was quiet, and it smelled like coffee and

chocolate, two of Hunter's favorite things. Of course, he brought them both with him every morning, and Lauren hardly spent any time here. He enjoyed the quiet, and the work, and the fact that he could take time off whenever he wanted.

Lauren had insisted on a family dinner at her house on Saturday night, and Hunter was just glad it wasn't up at the Mansion. She'd only invited Jaime and Mabel, but Hunter's father had said he couldn't get away with not inviting his parents. So his grandparents had been invited to.

They hadn't responded to the invitation, so no one knew if they'd come or not. Hunter hoped they wouldn't. Then he felt guilty for such things. No matter what, he had mixed feelings about the next three days.

When Alice dropped Westin off that night, he had a much bigger suitcase than normal. She held him extra-tight for an extra-long time, and Hunter saw the love in her eyes when she told him to have fun and be good.

Those were always her parting words to their son, and Hunter loved them. He did love her, and he got up from his spot at the table and followed her onto the porch. "Alice?" he asked, almost hesitantly as if she hadn't heard him and his cane following her.

It would be Valentine's Day next week, and he suddenly didn't want to spend it without her.

She hugged herself as she turned back to him. "Yeah?"

"Thank you for letting me have him for the whole weekend."

"Of course. Your parents are coming."

"I want you to come too." He inched forward and took her hand in his. "I know you're still upset with me about the road trip, but...I thought we were working toward being a family."

Her chin quivered the slightest bit, but she could've just been freezing. The wind was particularly nasty at the moment.

"Is that what you still want?" he asked.

She nodded, and he squeezed her hand. "All right, then. Dinner at Lauren and Trent's place tomorrow night. Five o'clock. You'll come?"

She glanced down the road to where their bigger house sat. "I'll think about it."

Hunter cradled her face in his palm, glad when she leaned into his touch. "Don't think too hard, sweetheart," he said, leaning down to kiss her. Finally, this kiss felt like the ones they'd been sharing before he'd messed up and driven for almost four hours in a single day just for a bowl of mashed potatoes.

She kissed him back with that same passion he'd come to expect, the maturity of a woman who knew what she wanted—and she wanted Hunter.

"I'm trying," she breathed, breaking their connection. "There's a lot for us to work through, you know?"

"Yeah," he said. "But isn't it easier when we do it

together? You don't have to do everything by yourself, Alice. Not anymore." The fact that she'd had to at all brought crippling guilt to his spine.

"I'm working on it." She pressed her lips to his again, and he let her take whatever she needed to from the kiss. By the time she pulled away, she was breathing heavily,, and she turned away from him quickly. "Have a good trip tomorrow."

"Thanks," he said, watching her practically fly down the front steps and into her car. He wondered what spooked her—him, or her own feelings about him.

No matter what it was, he hoped she'd figure out how to overcome it in the next forty-eight hours so she could come to dinner.

"THERE THEY ARE," HE SAID, POINTING AS HIS PARENTS finally emerged from the belly of the airport. His mother's dark hair had been recently colored so there was no gray showing. She carried her purse and a stuffed animal in one hand, pulling her suitcase with the other.

She scanned the waiting area, spotting Hunter quickly. She said something to his father, and they made a beeline for Hunter, Jaime, and Westin.

His parents both wore a grin the size of Texas on their faces when they finally pushed through the crowd.

"You must be Westin," his mother said, crouching

down and taking the boy by his shoulders. "Oh, I love you already." Tears spilled out of her eyes, and she drew him into her for a hug. "I love you already."

Hunter had a hard time swallowing, but he managed to hug his father hello and introduce him to Jaime before his mother backed up and let his dad have a turn. He looked right into Westin's face, and said, "Yep. You belong to us," before picking him up and hugging him.

"Grandpa has a bad back," Hunter said as Westin giggled. "Dad, you're going to hurt yourself."

"I am not," he said, settling Westin on his hip. "You're tiny, Westin. Are you sure you're eight?"

Westin laughed again, and he asked, "Is your name really Westin too?"

"That's right," his dad said. "Your mother named you after me."

"And Dad," Westin said.

"Your two names are reversed," his mother said. "He's Hunter Westin. You're Westin Hunter."

"What's your middle name, Grandpa?"

"Charles," he said. "My grandfather's name was Charles, so that became my middle name."

"I have a Charles in my class," Westin said. "He has a lizard."

"Wow, a lizard," his mom said as they started toward the exit.

"I have a hedgehog," Westin said. "And they're so much better than lizards."

Hunter chuckled, trailing behind as Jaime led the way back to the car. He didn't mind. From behind, he could see the adoration and love shining brightly in the way they looked at each other and then back to Westin. The boy really could talk about anything and everything for a really long time, and Hunter was very grateful for that.

They took Westin to the hotel pool, and bought Westin whatever he wanted for breakfast, and told Westin all about the beaches in Southern California. They merged right into his life, and Hunter was so grateful his parents were the people they were.

On Saturday, Westin went to Trent and Lauren's to play for a little bit while his parents went to visit their parents. The Quinns hailed from Bell Hill, and then they were stopping by the Magleby's on the way back.

Hunter fully expected to find his mother's eyes rimmed with red when they returned, but instead, he found himself trying to jump to his feet as his grandmother Magleby entered the cabin.

"Hunter," she said in a dignified voice, as if she was the Queen of England herself. "It's so good to see you."

Really? he wanted to squeak. He'd been back in town for quite a long while now, and she could clearly get around better than he did.

"Hey, Grandma," he said, hugging her gingerly. She barely touched him before backing up and glancing at his leg.

"Did I hurt you?" she asked.

"No," he said. "I'm all right."

"Mom, come sit down," his mother said, indicating the armchair in front of the window. "Hunter has a dog that can do the best tricks." She'd been trying to impress her mother-in-law for forty years now, and Hunter didn't think Clara could do any trick that could help with that.

"Oh, Granddad loved dogs." His grandmother sat down, and while she still wore a sharpness in her eyes, she was getting up there in years, just like Mabel. He wondered what dinner that evening would look like, as the two sisters finally got together in the same room. He wondered if Lauren had warned Aunt Mabel appropriately.

The afternoon wore on easily, as Westin returned and charmed everyone. When five o'clock hit, they all walked down the lane to Lauren's house.

It smelled like roasted meat and rosemary, and Hunter drew in a breath. Hopefully not his last good breath before a bomb exploded from everyone being in the same room. Hugs were exchanged, and the noise level grew as everyone got introduced to everyone else. Hunter found the end of the couch and sat down, his leg bothering him from the short walk.

Aunt Mabel and his sister hugged, and then she leaned in and said something to Hunter's grandmother that she clearly didn't like.

"Mom," he said, nodding toward the two Magleby sisters. Though the two older women were directly related to his father, his dad had never intervened in their arguments.

No, that had been his mother, and she'd been driven out of town because she couldn't get along with her husband's family.

His mom went over to find out what was going, and a few seconds later, she held up her hands as if to get them to both be quiet.

There was definite tension hanging in the air along with the scent of butter and cream from the mashed potatoes Lauren put on the counter beside a green cast iron pot with the lid still on. He really wanted to know what was in that pot—and so did Clara and all the other dogs. They sat in a line along the back of the kitchen, but their attention never went far from the food on the counter.

"What's going on?" he asked his father.

"The same thing that always goes on," he said, eyeing the situation near the stove. "Mabel and my mother don't get along. Your mother tries to help them understand that they're much too old to be acting like petty teenagers." He broadcast some bitterness in his words, and Hunter couldn't even begin to understand what he'd been through over the years.

"Why don't they get along?"

"I'm not sure either of them can remember anymore," he said. "But it was because of a man. One of my uncle's friends they both liked."

Hunter's insides turned to ice and then liquid. A man

had come to Mabel's weeks ago, claiming she'd left something for him. "Really? Who?"

"I don't know. Uncle Malachi had a lot of friends—and a lot of sisters." His dad shook his head and went over to the counter to get a soda. He held it up as if to ask Hunter if he wanted one, and he nodded.

"I invited Alice," he said when his father returned to his side. "That was probably a mistake, right?"

His dad swiveled his head toward him slowly, as if trying to find the location of an odd sound. "You invited Alice?"

Hunter took a long swig of his soda, instantly regretting it. He hated how the carbonation burned his throat, and he made a face and set the can on the side table beside the couch. "We're trying to make things work between us."

"What?" his father's question got drowned out by the sound of the doorbell ringing at the same time someone pounded on the front door.

It was enough to render everyone silent for some reason, and Hunter had the very bad feeling that that bomb was about to go off. He sat frozen on the couch, watching the three women across from him for their reaction. They'd all seized too.

"I'll get it," Westin said, skipping over to the door and opening it before anyone could stop him.

Two people stood there. One was Alice, and Hunter

thawed enough to push himself off the couch and grab his cane.

The other was the same man who'd stopped by Aunt Mabel's. Clyde...something. Hunter couldn't remember his name, but both he and Alice were triggers. They shouldn't be here. What had he been thinking?

"Look who I ran into," Alice said in a bright voice that Hunter couldn't tell was false or not. "Your aunt's boyfriend. We were both nervous about coming in, so we knocked and rang the bell together." She beamed at him, and then focused on Hunter still trying to get to them.

Mabel has a boyfriend? streamed through his mind as he limped forward. Behind him, Lauren said those exact words, her incredulity matching that flowing through Hunter.

"You're dating him again?" Siobhan practically screeched, providing the heat needed for the bomb to go off.

"She's here?" His mother's voice joined the fray. "Who invited her? Why is she here?"

"Hey," Hunter said, finally arriving in front of Alice and wrapping his fingers around the door, partially bringing it closed as if he could block out the arguing and exclamations still coming hard and fast behind him. He tried to smile, but he was about to get burned alive, and he knew first-hand what that felt like. No time to smile. No reason to smile.

"Uh, things are tense here," he said. "Maybe we should—"

"Come in," Lauren said, taking hold of the door and opening it wider where Hunter had tried to close it.

"Lauren," he hissed.

"It's time to just get it all out," she said. "Then we can just move on. All of us."

She wore a look of pure determination on her face, and Hunter had no choice but to back up a limp-step and said, "Come on in."

All he could do was hope he wasn't throwing Alice into a den of hungry lions.

18

Alice had no idea what she was walking into, but she kept a plastic smile cemented in place on her face. Lauren led them down the short hall and into the living space, which was mostly one big open room, with a kitchen on Alice's right and a living room on her left. Through the sliding glass doors in the back, there was a deck, and she wondered if it was as magnificent as the one at Trent's old house.

Two long tables had been set up in between the two spaces, and Alice felt like it was a line that had been drawn down the middle. She needed to pick a side.

"Alice and Clyde are here," Lauren announced before going into the kitchen, where Trent, Mabel Magleby and her sister Siobhan stood. None of them smiled or attended to any of the pots on the stove.

On the left, Hunter inched closer to who were clearly

his parents, just a bit older than Alice remembered them. The daggered look his mother shot in Alice's direction could've sliced her open had it been a blade.

What is she doing here?

Just because Alice had been standing on the threshold of the house didn't mean her ears had stopped working.

Porter and Westin stood almost right in front of her, clearly trying to decide which side to choose as well.

"Hey, Mabel," Clyde said easily, moving to the right and sweeping a kiss along the old woman's forehead. "Siobhan."

"I can't believe you would come here," Siobhan said. "After what you did...."

"He didn't do anything," Mabel said. "And you know it. You've just been blaming him for Gene's bad decision for years. Grow up, Siobhan."

Siobhan looked like she might cry, her face all crumpled up like that. Then she regained her composure and slid her icy mask back in place. "What do I care if you two see each other? She has one foot in the grave already." She walked away from Mabel and Clyde with as much grace as a ninety-year-old woman could.

"Better than living out of one for a decade," Mabel said quietly, but definitely loud enough for everyone to hear. She looked up at Clyde and slipped her weathered hand into his. The smile they exchanged might be kind of wobbly, but it was there nonetheless.

Alice had never known Mabel Magleby to date. Or to

have ever gone on a date. Or even thought about having a boyfriend. Her heart took courage at the older couple, thinking there was always time for a second chance.

Her eyes flew to Hunter, where he stood next to his parents—more Magleby's and Magleby drama. "Alice, I'm sure you remember my mother and father."

"Of course," she said, moving forward to greet them. His father shook her hand, but his mother simply stared at her, and Alice didn't dare hug her or touch her.

"You had a baby and didn't say anything?" she said, each word louder than the last. "Who does that?"

"Mom," Hunter said, almost under his breath.

"No, really," Darlene continued. "I want to know why I had to meet my grandson in an airport when he was almost nine years old."

Of course she did. And she'd want a really good reason. Alice didn't have one of those, and she looked helplessly at Hunter.

Who stood there, mute.

"I—" She opened her mouth to speak, but she had no reason. Westin moved over to his paternal grandmother and put his hand in hers. A surge of emotion roared up Alice's throat at the simple gesture, and she couldn't identify all the moving parts of her feelings.

"It's okay, Grandma," he said in his little boy voice before he turned to face Alice. She felt like they'd all ganged up on her, and a lump formed in her throat that brought tears to her eyes.

"You've got nothing to say to us?" Darlene demanded, and her husband touched her arm.

"Darlene," he said. "You're making a scene."

"Am I?" she screeched. "Well, someone has to, and it won't be you. I'm tired of being the one who says nothing." She glanced into the kitchen, where everyone stood watching. Even the dogs had riveted their attention on Hunter's mother.

"Siobhan, you didn't even like Clyde by the time he asked out Mabel. Did you know she'd already gone out with Gene three times before she even broke up with you?" She shook her head, pure disgust in her expression. "So if there's anyone to blame for the past, it's you, Siobhan."

"He stole Gene's insurance company," Siobhan said.

"No, *Gene* made dumb decision after dumb decision." Darlene swiped at her eyes. "And he went bankrupt five years before he even told you." She glared lasers at her mother-in-law. "So Aunt Mabel is right, Siobhan. It's time to let go. Move on. Accept that you made a mistake in the past, and that your husband wasn't perfect."

"I know he wasn't perfect."

"And yet, you drove me out of town." Darlene's voice carried so much bitterness, indicating so much history that Alice didn't know about.

"Honey," her husband said. "It's okay."

"No, it is not okay." She looked wild, and Alice felt true fear for a moment. Hunter stepped in front of his mom and said something Alice couldn't hear. She nodded and calmed down, wiping her eyes furiously now.

"Grandma."

"Yes, Westin?" She dropped into a crouch that put them at the same height, and her love for her grandson outshone the sun. Pure guilt hit Alice hard in the gut, and she turned away from the scene.

She couldn't help feeling like she didn't belong here, with this family that belonged only to Hunter. But *she* wanted to belong to Hunter, too. She'd made mistakes—a lot of mistakes, and she didn't want to be faced with them so clearly.

Moving quickly, she took the few steps toward the front door, knowing Hunter would not be able to keep up with her. She yanked open the door and left the house, the air outside crisp, with the scent of rain hanging in it.

Her tears splashed down her face as she flew down the steps, and the only thing that stopped her was Hunter calling her name.

She turned back to see him at the top of the steps, making his way down. "Don't go," he said. "We can work it out."

"She *hates* me," she sobbed, and Hunter put his hand on her shoulder, steadying her.

"Your parents hated me," he reminded her softly. "They just need some time. They haven't had much time to absorb the fact that Westin exists."

Alice shook her head wildly, so desperate to get out

of there that she couldn't think straight. "And you said nothing. You didn't even come to my side. You just let her...." She shook her head. Everything that had happened since she'd married Hunter Magleby had gone wrong. Her throat burned as her breath hitched in her chest.

It had all gone wrong, and that was because of her. Her fault. Her mistakes. Her silence.

"I have to go." She turned away from him, his hand dropping off her shoulder.

"Come on," he said, a hint of annoyance in his voice as she walked away.

But she couldn't go back inside. As she got behind the wheel of her car, she saw Mabel and Clyde standing on the porch, watching her, and Hunter glaring at her with all the force of a hurricane.

She didn't care. She just started her car, put it in reverse, and put Forgotten Road—and Hunter Magleby— in her rearview mirror.

HOURS LATER, ALICE'S CAR NEEDED GAS, OR SHE'D FIND herself stranded on the side of the road in the middle of... stranded somewhere in Washington. She had two more nights without Westin. Another day. She could find a hotel and figure things out.

Of course, by then Westin and Darlene Magleby

would be gone, and maybe her life could go back to normal.

Problem was, she didn't even know what normal was anymore. Sleeping all day, working all night, seeing Westin for a few hours before driving him across town to his father's? Sure, they'd settled into a routine, but it was not one Alice would choose for life.

Every time she thought of Hunter just standing there, saying nothing, her jaw would tighten and her foot would press on the accelerator a little harder. How could he not have defended her? Weren't they supposed to be a team?

He's not your husband, she told herself for the umpteenth time. But they'd talked about making a family again. Being better co-parents. Being on the same page. Back at that house, he'd been part of another book, and Alice couldn't believe he'd even invited her in the first place.

She pulled into a gas station and started filling up her car. Night had fallen long ago, and she looked up at the stars winking in the sky above her. She felt like one of them.

Far away.

Isolated from everything and everyone.

Trying to shine light into the vast darkness, but hardly making a dent at all.

Helplessness and desperation welled up in her throat as she got behind the wheel and started driving again.

Forty minutes later, she finally spotted a hotel and

pulled in. Once she had paid and gotten her key, she pushed into the tiny, dark box of a room and shut the door behind her. A sigh leaked from her body, taking with it some of her exhaustion and anguish.

She'd sleep first. Then, in the morning, she'd figure out a plan for how she and Hunter could live in Hawthorne Harbor together—parent their son together—without ever having to talk to one another again.

On Monday evening, she didn't get out of the car in front of Hunter's cabin. "You go on in," she said to Westin, watching the front door like it might explode open at any moment. "I love you. See you tomorrow after school."

"Bye, Mom." He got out and ran up the steps to the door. By the time he opened it, Alice had the sedan in reverse and was backing out.

They hadn't talked about the party on Saturday night. For once, Westin had simply said the weekend was great, and then he'd launched into something about an art project they'd be starting next month.

Alice drove home, her phone ringing twice along the way. When Hunter called the third time, she picked it up.

"So you're not going to come in anymore?" he asked by way of greeting.

"Nope," Alice said, popping the P on the word.

"Alice," he said. "I thought we were—"

"Well, we're not," she said, wondering if she could take the night off. She wasn't sure how she'd even done the most basic of things that day, like shower and get dressed. But she wasn't naked, so she must've done it.

"Why not?"

"Because, Hunter," she said very clearly and very slowly. A strange calm came over her. "You made it very clear which side you were on at the party. And it's not mine."

"Alice—"

"Good-bye, Hunter." She hung up, her heart caving in on itself at the same time she burst into tears.

19

Hunter growled through everything he did after Alice hung up on him. He spent Valentine's Day in his cabin with Westin and two cupcakes from the bakery he'd managed to get during his lunch break. He'd stood in line for almost the whole hour, but he didn't want the highlight of his son's day to be the lame cards his classmates had passed out.

Unfortunately, Westin was equally excited by everything, so the cupcakes stood on the same ground as the store-bought cards from the kids at school. At least Hunter hadn't been alone, even if he'd stared out the window, thinking Alice's headlights would sweep through the darkness when she arrived.

That didn't happen, and he let Westin stay up until he fell asleep on the couch. The fact that Hunter couldn't carry his son down the hall to bed made him even growlier.

Hour by hour, day by day, time passed. Files and receipts got put in the computer and filed in the cabinet. He ordered his groceries and got them delivered. He made sure Westin's homework was done, and the boy was ready to go on time for Alice's mother.

She still came up to the door, but Hunter always busied himself with dishes or feeding Clara when she did. Then all he had to do was wave with a sudsy hand or nod at her as he bent down to put the dog food in the bowl.

She'd never been chatty, and he thought he'd done a pretty good job of hiding how surly he was.

Until one day, she said, "You go wait with Grandpa, Westie. I need to talk to your dad."

Hunter turned from where he was washing and re-washing Westin's cereal bowl, his heart pounding in the back of his throat. Karen stepped toward him, an edge in her eyes he didn't like. One he'd seen before, too.

She'd worn this look when she'd come over to his apartment a few days before he and Alice had gotten married. She'd told him he couldn't marry her daughter, and she'd begged him to give it some time.

"Six months," Karen had said. "A year. If you're in love now, you will be then."

If only Hunter had listened to her then. He rinsed the bowl and his hands and faced Karen. "What's up?"

She peered up and into his face. "You look tired, Hunter."

"Thank you," he said, only a hint of dryness in his voice. He plucked a towel from the counter and turned away.

"Alice is miserable."

"I don't care," he said.

"Oh, come on," she said, putting her hand on his shoulder. He shrugged it off as he spun toward her again. She fell back a step, his anger putting an invisible balloon between them.

"Karen," he said as calmly as possible, his Marine training kicking in. "Alice and I aren't really talking right now, and I don't need a lecture from you."

"I know what's going on with you and Alice."

"You always did," he said, his voice bitter. Alice was upset that Hunter hadn't been on her side. He'd been frozen by his mother's outburst at the party. As soon as Alice had left, a lot of the tension had subsided. His grandmother sulked through most of the meal, but she didn't cause any other problems for Aunt Mabel and Clyde.

Hunter hadn't known what to do. What to say. Where to stand. And he'd obviously done them all wrong in her eyes.

But she wasn't exactly on the same page with him either. She'd always confided more in her mother than in him, and he wasn't sure what had possessed him to think they had a second chance at being a family.

"She'd welcome you back," Karen said. "That's all I'm saying." She turned and went toward the front door.

Hunter scoffed as the door closed. "Welcome me back. That's insane." She'd hung up on him, and then refused to answer any of his texts and calls. True, he'd only tried a couple of times, but Hunter had never been one to beg.

Alice had made her feelings clear. He had to respect that. Didn't he?

He got in the shower and waited at the bottom of the steps for Lauren to drive him over to the office. She puttered around with him for an hour or so before going to a job site, but thankfully, she didn't bring up Alice.

"See you tonight," she said as she grabbed her sunglasses from the top of the filing cabinet.

"I might not need a ride home," he said. "I'll let you know."

She turned back from the door. "You okay?"

"I've got a headache," he said. Westin wasn't coming over that night, and Hunter thought maybe he could go home early and get some sleep.

"Well, let me know. I have that meeting for the Spring Fling, and then I'm going up to the Mansion, so I'll be going that way in a couple of hours."

"All right." Hunter went back to the bank statement, a slip of pain behind his eyes that he wished he could get rid of.

"Have you talked to Alice?" Lauren asked.

"No," he said.

"Maybe you should—"

"Why is everyone trying to get me to talk to Alice?" he asked. "I tried talking to her. She made it very clear she didn't want to talk to me. Is that what women what? A man who doesn't respect what they say?" His chest heaved, and he wasn't sure when he'd become so desperate for Lauren to leave. Or maybe he was desperate for Alice to contact him. Just come in for a minute when she dropped off Westin. Text him back. Anything.

He wasn't sure.

"I'm sorry," Lauren said. "I won't bother you about her."

"Thank you," Hunter said, and Lauren ducked out the door. Hunter looked at the screen again, but he couldn't remember where he was. He tried to focus on a different task, but his thoughts kept derailing him back to Alice.

Always back to Alice.

He finally got up and left the office, the sun shining brightly today, as March only sat a day or two away. He walked to the corner, the downtown park where a lot of town activities directly across the street.

The Lavender Festival took over the park every July, and his first thought was how he'd connected with Alice the summer after they'd graduated right there in that park. He checked both ways before crossing the street, a bit of comfort seeping into him the moment he stepped onto the sidewalk in the park.

He hadn't missed a single physical therapy appointment, and while his leg never felt quite right, he could walk pretty well now. So he walked around the entire park and then into the statue in the center. He could practically smell the lavender in the air and taste the concoctions people came up with for the cook-off.

He'd never liked the crowds, and this morning was peaceful and calm. Hunter found a bench and relaxed into it, feeling more stuck than he ever had.

Maybe he should get out of town for the rest of the day. Get in the car and go somewhere. Even up to the lodge at the Olympic Park would get Hawthorne Harbor out of his head.

He didn't think he could go anywhere far enough to get Alice out of his head. And he couldn't drive anywhere by himself anyway.

A sense of helplessness filled him from top to bottom, and the headache behind his eyes throbbed painfully.

He'd just gotten up to leave when a man in a wheelchair entered the park. He was alone, like Hunter, and Hunter couldn't help watching him for a moment. He wondered how long he'd been in the wheelchair and whether or not he worked alone in an office and had perpetual pain in his legs.

Even as he watched, a little girl called to him, and she came running over to him from the playground. A woman came with her, a smile on her face, and the little girl catapulted herself into the man's lap. He laughed, and the picture before Hunter was so full of family, and so perfect that Hunter couldn't help wanting it for himself.

He pulled out his phone and called Aunt Mabel. "Hello, Hunter," she said in a raspy voice like he'd just woken her. "I have a bride with me. You have five seconds."

"I need a ride up to the lodge at Olympic Park."

"Jaime is busy all day."

Hunter's hopes fell even further, but he didn't look to his left. He didn't want to see that picture-perfect family's happiness. Not when he couldn't have it himself.

"Call Adam Herrin," she said.

"Why?"

"Just do it," Aunt Mabel barked, and the line went dead. Hunter sighed, unsure of what to do. Aunt Mabel had her finger on the pulse of the entire town, and if she said to call the Chief of Police, he should probably do it.

He looked up the police department's website and called the non-emergency number. "Adam Herrin, please," he said when the receptionist answered.

After a few more questions, Hunter finally just said, "Look, my aunt told me to call him, okay? If he's too busy, can you just have him call me back?"

A moment of silence passed, and then the woman said, "Hold, please."

It seemed like forever before the Chief came on and

said, "Adam Herrin," in a somewhat barky voice. Hunter knew such a tone well. He didn't think anyone in the Marines spoke in soft tones, and Hunter didn't flinch at all.

"Adam, it's Hunter Magleby. My aunt said to call you, because I need a ride up to the lodge at Olympic Park."

"Today?"

"If possible."

"When can you go?"

"Anytime," he said. He'd only stay overnight, and he didn't need to pack a bag to stay somewhere for less than twenty-four hours. He'd definitely gone for much longer than that without running water and a toothbrush, and maybe the forest would clear his head.

"My wife's leaving in an hour to go to work. She works up there."

Apprehension coursed through Hunter. He didn't know Adam Herrin's wife, and he didn't want to spend the drive trying to make small talk.

"If you want a ride, I'll let her know," Adam said, his voice definitely gentler now.

"Yes," Hunter said, deciding on the spot. "I'm at the park downtown. She can just pick me up there."

"I'll let her know."

Satisfied and feeling somewhat hopeful, Hunter glanced over to where the family had been a few minutes ago. They were gone, but it wasn't hard to spot them down the sidewalk in the parking lot.

He watched in disbelief as the little girl got in the backseat while the mother helped her husband get behind the wheel. She folded the chair easily and lifted it into the trunk before going around to the passenger door.

How was that man going to drive? Hunter's mind fired like a twenty-one gun salute, and he needed to get somewhere with the Internet, because a new door had just opened right before his eyes.

THE FOREST THAT SURROUNDED THE LODGE AT OLYMPIC Park smelled like pine needles and rain, though the last storm had come through a couple of days ago.

Hunter loved it, breathed it deeply into his soul. There were a few easy trails out to a couple of plaques, and Hunter walked out to them, the sun helping to shine light into the dark parts of his mind.

When he returned to the lodge, he found a coffee mixer happening in the fireplace area. He normally didn't drink too much caffeine in the evening, but he decided to stay because there weren't many people hanging out and the scent of dark roast called to him.

A couple each held a mug and perched on the hearth, only a few feet from Hunter in the armchair. He was comfortable, and he let his eyes drift closed, not intending to eavesdrop. But there was soft music playing and not much chatter, so he could easily hear them.

"I just want you to be happy," the man said.

"I am happy."

"I don't think you are."

Silence came after that, and Hunter didn't mind it. *I just want you to be happy.*

He wanted Alice to be happy.

He wanted to be happy himself.

He wanted Westin to be happy. Everyone else...Hunter would help them if he could, but most of his mental energy and time went to Alice and Westin.

Karen had said Alice was miserable, and Hunter was well-acquainted with that feeling. In fact, this level of discontentment and unhappiness was exactly what he'd been expecting to feel in Hawthorne Harbor.

But he wasn't in Hawthorne Harbor tonight, and he needed to figure out how to live there and be happy.

He knew what he needed. Or rather, whom.

He needed Alice.

20

Alice drove away from Hunter's cabin without seeing him for the sixteenth time, her mouth set in a determined line. Determined not to cry. Determined not to turn around and go back.

Hey, at least she wasn't crying. The tears had dried up a few days ago, but they hit her at random times still, especially if Westin said something about Hunter or asked her something about his father.

Spring was coming to Hawthorne Harbor, but it didn't feel like quite the rebirth that it usually did. She made it through her shifts with the aid of her friends and a lot of diet cola. Dr. Murphy had finally returned, and he'd sat them down for a staff meeting to explain his health scare and concerns.

"But I'm okay," he'd said. "They got the tumor, and I'm undergoing light chemotherapy."

But Alice knew there was no such thing as "light" chemotherapy. He looked worn right around the edges, the same way Alice did.

She was on the late shift tonight, so she didn't actually have to go in until eleven. She drove past the pier and into town, wondering what to do with herself until she had to go to work. She still had a love-hate relationship with dropping Westin off at Hunter's in the evenings. Most of the time, she enjoyed a few minutes alone to go shopping or grab herself a chicken sandwich.

But since she'd stopped talking to Hunter, the only thing she'd experienced was loneliness. It seemed to crowd in on her, pressing against her chest and back until she felt sure she'd suffocate.

She drew in a deep breath as she passed all the iconic downtown buildings on Main Street. The library, the downtown park, the fire station. The Anchor, the bed & breakfast, the city office buildings, Gretchen's flower shop, all of it.

Alice had lived here for most of her life, and though she'd gone to British Columbia for a brief time, she felt like she'd never left Hawthorne Harbor. Had never wanted to leave.

But now...she exhaled as she turned onto the road that would lead her out to the Lavender Highway. She wouldn't be going that far, though. No, she turned into Duality, the thriving, always busy convenience store that offered everything from gas to the best breakfast burritos on the planet.

They wouldn't have the ham, cheese, and egg delights this late in the day, but they had plenty of other hot food to choose from. She picked out a pesto pasta pizza and a box of tater tots, not caring about the carbs today.

She hadn't for a while now, since deciding that if she couldn't have Hunter, she didn't want anyone. After moving her car to a further parking space, she sat behind the wheel and ate, feeling adrift in a huge world where nothing made sense.

Her phone rang, reminding her that she wasn't completely alone. Sadie and Angela at the hospital had made sure she felt loved by bringing her candy and soda and hugging her at least once during every shift.

They'd cried with her and talked to her about Hunter, but they were no replacement for the man who'd stolen her heart a decade ago, taken it with him when he left town, and now held it hostage.

"Hey, Mom," she said, trying to sound upbeat. Her voice just sounded false.

"Where are you? I thought you'd be home for a few hours. Aren't you going in late tonight?"

"I stopped to get something to eat," she said. Her relationship with her mom teetered on rocky ground at the moment, because while she knew of Alice's and Hunter's problems, all she did was talk about how wonderful

Hunter was. It was almost like she wanted to rub salt in Alice's open and bleeding wounds.

"Westin said he tried to call you," she said. "I guess he left something at home he needs for tomorrow."

"He didn't call," she said. He didn't even have a phone, which meant he would've used Hunter's, and Alice would've had a heart attack had any calls come from that number.

"You didn't block Hunter's number?"

"Mom," Alice said with a sigh. "I drop my son off there every time I go to work. You think I blocked the only phone number that can be used to get in touch with me should something happen?" What kind of mother did her mom think she was?

It didn't matter. Alice carried plenty of guilt about what kind of mother she was.

"No, of course not. I'm being silly."

"So he called you? What does he need?"

"Yes, he said he left his shoes for his wax museum costume."

Alice sighed in a long, exaggerated way. She hated the big projects at school—like the wax museum. Westin had chosen LeBron James, and he had to have the huge shoes to go with the basketball clothes.

"Fine," she said. "I'll take them over there when I'm done here." She didn't add that she'd asked Westin three times if he'd had all the pieces of his costume for school the next day.

"Where are you?"

"Almost done," she said, not wanting to admit she'd eaten dinner alone in a parking lot. "Talk to you later." The call ended, and Alice could've left right away. But she didn't. Instead, she navigated to her gallery and started sifting through the pictures stored on her phone.

Her eyes filled with tears as she went through the photos of Westin over the years. Yes, they'd been alone, but they'd always had each other. He'd given her a reason to get up in the morning and go to school, finish her classes, get to work on time. He depended on her, and if she didn't do something, no one would.

Now, with Hunter in the picture, Alice felt obsolete. Unnecessary. And in fact, unwanted.

She leaned her head back and let the tears track down her face. "Why doesn't Hunter want me?"

She'd asked that question a lot after he'd left and she'd annulled their marriage. That question was one she never wanted her baby to ask, and it became a major reason she'd decided to keep Westin and raise him herself.

Only now she didn't have to do everything herself—if only she could figure out how to get on the same ground as Hunter.

She drew in a deep breath and wiped her eyes. "Common ground. We need common ground."

They really were opposites in a lot of ways, but they'd always have one thing in common—Westin.

Alice seized onto her son, her mind firing on all cylinders now. She was so *tired*, and it was hard to think.

But she knew one thing—Westin did need her, and it was time to stop acting like a martyr. She needed to stop feeling sorry for herself too. Her aunt Patty had told her that almost ten years ago.

"You made these choices. Now stop feeling sorry for yourself and do what you think will be best."

Those words had guided young Alice so often in the first few years of Westin's life. They'd pointed her toward nursing school and back to Hawthorne Harbor.

Not every decision she'd made had been the best, but she'd done the best she could, at that time, with what she knew.

An image of Darlene's horrified, puckered up face flashed through her mind. She'd definitely made some mistakes there, and she hadn't gotten the chance to apologize. She should've apologized at the party. Why hadn't she apologized?

Everything had fallen apart so quickly, and Alice still needed some time to sort through the debris. But she could—and would—apologize to Hunter's parents. She'd need their phone number or an address where she could send a letter. The easiest source to get those things would be Hunter himself.

She wasn't sure she could ask him for anything right now. A plan formed in her head as she returned quickly to her house, grabbed Westin's basketball shoes, and drove back to Forgotten Road. She put the shoes on the front porch and knocked, turning to leave immediately.

She'd reached the bottom of the steps when Westin said, "Thanks, Mom," into the gathering darkness.

"You're welcome, bud," she said. The rectangle of light disappeared as the door swung closed, and Alice stared at it. She should've known Hunter wouldn't come to the door. He even had a dog who could open it and bring in the shoes herself.

Foolishness hit her, and she almost abandoned her plan. She clung to it though, needing to do something that felt like a step in the right direction.

So she went back to the main road and on up to Magleby Mansion. She'd have to walk, but she didn't want to drive all the way back down and around to get to Mabel's house. And besides, she had time and the Mansion was well lit.

By the time she knocked on Mabel's door, her plan had disintegrated in her mind. When Mabel opened the door, she simply stood there and stared at Alice. No smile. No hello.

She finally said, "It's about time," and stepped back to let Alice enter the house.

Alice stepped inside, because Mabel was her lifeline to Hunter's parents. And his parents were her lifeline to Hunter.

And she had to do something to get to where Hunter was.

ANOTHER WEEK PASSED BEFORE ALICE'S ROUTINE GOT interrupted again. She'd been busy making calls and texts and arranging to get work off so she could drive to Seattle and pick up Darlene and Westin at the airport.

At times, it had seemed impossible that any of it would come together, and yet, by some miracle, it had.

She dropped Westin off at Hunter's as normal—neither of them knew about Alice's secret meeting with Hunter's parents.

"They don't need to know yet," she muttered to herself, something she'd been doing a lot this week. It seemed like she had to tell herself everything out loud before she could believe it.

Thankfully, Darlene had answered the phone, just as Mabel had said she would. Alice had apologized for her actions so long ago, and she'd invited his parents to sit down and talk to her.

Just her.

Her hands tightened on the steering wheel as she left town, her nerves vibrating with the speed of humming-bird wings.

She'd offered to go to San Diego—which would've been much harder and cost much more. But she'd been willing to do anything they wanted.

They said they'd come to her, because then they could see Westin again.

So they had tonight to meet, and in the morning, she'd drive them back to Hawthorne Harbor. Hunter knew they were coming—his mother had told him that much. But she'd fibbed and said they'd rent a car and get themselves to his house.

By the time she parked and walked into the airport, Alice felt like throwing up. All she could see was Darlene's blotchy face as she aired dirty laundry at the party. Though they'd talked a few times this week and she'd been calm and kind, Alice had no idea what to expect when they came past security.

She saw Hunter's father first, and he looked so much like Hunter and Westin that Alice's chest hitched. Those Magleby's had such strong genes, and she'd always loved the unique color of Hunter's eyes.

"Alice," he said, his smile warm and genuine. He hugged her this time, letting go quickly so Darlene could face her.

Tears flooded Alice's eyes, and everything she'd even thought about saying fled. "Darlene, I'm so sorry." She grabbed onto her and held her tight, her whole body shaking as she cried.

Darlene cried too, and Alice said in a high-pitched voice, "I hope you can find a way to forgive me someday."

She didn't expect things to happen overnight, but she knew better than most that time did heal some wounds, and forgiveness could be found for most things.

Darlene stepped back, nodded, and wiped her eyes.

"I'm working on it." She glanced at her husband. "I'm so glad you called." She situated her purse and started toward the exit with her carryon rolling behind her. "Hunter's been so upset with me, and I didn't know how to reach out to you."

Surprise darted through Alice. "He's been upset with you? Why?"

"For driving you away at the party," Darlene said, looking at Alice. "He blames himself for a lot of things, and he's particularly stubborn about most of it. But yes, he's been upset with me."

Alice wanted to hear more about that, but she didn't want to pry. Maybe Hunter had stood up for her. Maybe he'd said things to his parents in her defense.

Doesn't matter, she told herself. She was going to explain to them why she'd done what she had, and they could either accept it or not. No matter what, she'd be one step closer to Hunter by morning.

21

"Morning," Hunter said as he went down the steps. He shook hands with Joseph, the man the Marines had sent to help Hunter learn how to drive using just his hands.

"Ready?" Joseph asked, a smile on his wide face. He'd never treated Hunter as anything but an able-bodied human, and Hunter appreciated him so much.

"I think so," Hunter said.

"Because we're moving today. You'll be driving." He beamed at Hunter like he'd just announced that Hunter had won a major award, not that he'd be doing something almost everyone could do.

A slip of unease ran through Hunter. "I'm ready," he said with more determination. He'd been doing lessons with Joseph for a week now, and he was actually surprised at how quickly the Marines had responded to his request for driving assistance and a hand-controlled vehicle.

"So get in, and let's go over a few things." Joseph moved over to the passenger side of the car, and Hunter went to the driver's side. His pulse hammered in his chest, and he took a deep breath to calm himself.

"Remember, the trickiest part is not trying to use your feet at all," Joseph said. "The pedals are still there, so it's possible. But you don't need to use your feet."

"Got it." Hunter had heard that same lesson every time he got in the car. He knew to pull was to push on the accelerator. He had to have some decent mobility and dexterity in his right hand and arm to keep pressure on the accelerator, pulling it toward him, and he'd been thanking God for a straight week that his arms had been unaffected in the explosion that had injured his leg, knee, and hip.

He pushed the lever away from him to brake, and he was worried about the pressure needed for that.

"It's just like using your feet," he said. "Little motions go a long way. We don't slam on the brakes, and we don't need to yank or press on the hand controls."

Hunter put his left hand on the wheel in a normal position. He could still operate the turn signal from this side, and he could use his right for the windshield wipers and the radio—as long as he was stopped.

Because he'd be using his right hand to operate the pedals on the floor. He didn't have leg spasms, so he didn't have a plate covering up the pedals, as Joseph had warned him. He could get one, as the dealership that had installed the permanent hand controls had told him.

But for now, he had a handle poking out on the right side of the steering wheel that looked like a regular mountain bike handle. He put his right hand on that, pushing and pulling to get a feel for the grip of it.

"All right," Joseph said. "Start 'er up, and let's see if we can back out."

Hunter liked how Joseph always acted like he was part of Hunter's team. He always used "we" and not "you," making Hunter feel less alone.

A twinge of emotion hit him in the chest, but he ignored it. He wasn't alone, even if he missed Alice in a way that made him ache. He was learning to drive, and once he knew how, he'd be showing up at her house and begging her to take him back.

He turned the key in the ignition like normal. No one walking by the car would know it was for a handicapped driver, and anyone could drive it. He'd asked for the option, and the dealership had done it. The Marines had paid for all of the mobility installation, after Hunter had bought the car. That had taken the most time, and then Joseph had shown up with the car and his driving lessons.

"So we put it in reverse as normal," Joseph said. "And then pull on that gas."

Hunter did as he said, and the car started to back up slowly. He burst out laughing, the elation coursing through him too much to contain. "I can't believe it," he said, though he'd watched videos of other handicapped people driving their cars. "I just can't believe it."

He turned the wheel so the car was facing the highway, and he put the vehicle in drive. Then he pulled slowly toward him again, and the car moved down the lane. "This is literally the best thing that ever happened to me."

He beamed at Joseph, who smiled right on back. "This is great, Hunter. You're going to be able to do everything you want now."

He nodded, his emotions suddenly too much for him to manage. He turned left and went up the road to the Mansion, where he signaled and turned in. After pulling to a stop right in front of the doors, he got out and hobbled up the steps. He'd told Aunt Mabel he had a surprise for her that morning, and she said she was working at the Mansion that day.

Before he reached the top of the steps, she opened the door and came out. "Hunter," she said, her eyes glued to the normal white sedan he'd purchased by looking at pictures online. "What is going on?"

"I can drive, Aunt Mabel. Come go for a ride." He peered behind her. "Where's Jaime?"

"He's coming in from the gardens now," she said, finally tearing her eyes from the car to look at him. "You can really drive that thing?"

"It has hand controls, Aunt Mabel." Hunter laughed

again. "And the military paid to have them installed." He waved at Joseph to get out, which he did. "This is Joseph Milan. He's been teaching me how to drive with my hands."

"Well, I'll be." Aunt Mabel moved down the steps and shook Joseph's hand. Jamie arrived, and Hunter told him the same thing.

Once everyone was loaded in, Hunter behind the wheel, he said, "Okay, let's go get some breakfast."

And he drove everyone down off the bluff and into town, the radio playing and people talking. As he waited for his plate of bacon and eggs, he couldn't help feeling like he'd just accomplished something great.

Something *really* great.

Gratitude overcame him, and he looked out the window to see that spring was definitely on its way. He pulled out his phone and texted his mother. *I can come get you on Wednesday morning.*

They were flying in for another visit, and he hadn't been sure if he'd be able to drive at the time. But he knew he could now. Yes, Seattle was a two-hour drive. But he could do it. He knew he could.

We'll be fine, she texted back. Your dad wants a car so we can get around.

Hunter hesitated to tell her he had a car now. Half of him wanted to surprise his parents with his newfound driving ability, the same way he was planning to do so with Alice. In the end, though, he decided to tell her, because he needed her help with what he had planned for Alice.

I have a car, he sent to her. You can drive it whenever you want.

You have a car?

And I can drive it, he texted. I'll have Jaime take a video and send it to you.

His food arrived, and he fired off one last text. *At breakfast. I'll call you later.* Then he put his phone away and joined the conversation at his table.

And the best part?

He drove everyone home afterward.

WEDNESDAY MORNING CAME, AND ALONG WITH IT, Hunter's nerves. Today was the day he'd talk to Alice again. Even if she didn't speak back to him, he'd get to see her, be in the same space as her, breathe in the scent of her skin. He'd almost forgotten what she sounded like, smelled like, looked like.

It had been almost five weeks from the disastrous party, and last week when Westin had forgotten some shoes, she'd come to the door and knocked and then ran away. Hunter had watched it all through the window, and he still wasn't sure she'd even allow him inside her house.

But he was going to try.

He couldn't keep living the way he was.

Westin ate breakfast as normal, but he wasn't going to school. His parents should've landed thirty minutes ago, and they'd be here by ten. The time seemed to pass slowly and quickly at the same time, and before he knew it, he heard the crunch of tires on the dirt road out front.

As he got up and said, "Grandma and Grandpa are here," a car door slammed. Westin bolted off the couch where he'd been playing a game on his tablet, and Clara followed him to the front door.

The boy opened it and ran outside, calling, "Grandma, Grandpa!" but Clara waited on the front porch for Hunter. He arrived and froze, taking in the scene before him.

Alice was there, standing with his parents as they hugged Westin. She hugged their son too, and then all four pairs of eyes moved to him.

"Alice?" the word sort of fell out of him, coated heavily in disbelief.

"Come show us your car," his mother called, but Hunter didn't move. All of his plans were ruined. He was supposed to show up at Alice's house with flowers and food and so many apologies she wouldn't be able to stay mad at him.

But she'd come here instead. With his parents.

"Dad, come on," Westin called.

Hunter got himself moving down the steps, Clara at his side. He only had eyes for Alice, and she couldn't seem to look away from him either. He hugged his parents and then came face-to-face with the woman he loved.

"I'm—" He cleared his throat. "It's great to see you."

She smiled, and it shook a little on her face. He grabbed onto her and drew her into a hug, so many things storming through him that he'd forgotten about his rehearsed speech and carefully crafted apologies.

"I'm sorry," he whispered into her hair. "Can we please, *please* try again?"

She nodded, and Hunter's whole world came to life in real color again. He blinked, and it was as if he'd been reborn right there in front of his cabin. He cleared his throat and stepped back from Alice, stumbling a bit.

His father grabbed onto his arm to steady him, an action that would've infuriated Hunter a couple of months ago. But now, he just flashed his father a thankful look and said, "So I bought a car, and I can drive it."

"You can not," his mother said. "How? Show us?"

"The Marines have a partnership with mobility experts all over the country," he said. "And there was a dealership out of Tacoma that fitted the car with hand controls." He opened the driver's door and moved out of the way. "So I can drive."

He met Alice's eye as his parents crowded into the space to look inside the car. "I had this great surprise planned for you. I was going to get dinner and show up at your house, and you'd be like, 'How'd you get here?' and I'd point to the car, and...." His voice trailed off, because she'd started weeping.

"I'm sorry," she said through her tears. "I've been

trying to get to where you are for weeks, and it seems like you were trying to get to where I was."

Hunter swallowed back the emotion in his throat. "I can take care of you and Westin."

"Of course you can," she said, stepping forward as if they were alone and cupping his face in her palm. "I've never doubted that."

"I don't want to saddle you with my injury," he said. "But I can do everything now."

She smiled and nodded. "I called your mom last week, and we've been talking."

Shock flowed through Hunter, and he looked at his mother. She watched him, her own tears making a path down her cheeks. She stepped over to Hunter and Alice, making the third side of a triangle.

"You two love each other so much. Work things out." She glanced at her husband. "Come on Westin. Let's take our grandson to the beach."

"It's not warm enough for the beach," Hunter said automatically, but they left anyway. He opened the back door of his car and pulled out the only thing he had ready for Alice—a case of Diet Coke.

"This was going to be part of the surprise," he said.

She looked at it and then him and burst out laughing.

"I thought you might need a lot of soda to deal with me again," he said, setting it on top of the sedan.

"Hunter." She stepped into his arms and swayed with him. "I'd do anything to have to deal with you again."

"Yeah?" He gazed down at her, his speech returning to his memory. "I'm in love with you, Alice Kopp. I've never stopped loving you, and I'm absolutely miserable without you."

She grinned and tipped up onto her toes as her eyes drifted closed. "I love you too, Hunter," she murmured just before she kissed him.

He kissed her in a way he only had a few times before, and she kissed him back with as much passion and love in her touch as he tried to put into his.

After a few minutes, he asked, "So do you want to go for a ride?"

To her eternal credit she said, "I thought you'd never ask."

22

———

Alice watched as Hunter used his right hand to make the car accelerate and stop. "This is amazing," she said.

"I feel like myself again," he said, glancing at her. "That might sound weird, but it's how I feel."

"I can see why," she said, and she could. She couldn't imagine not being able to do simple things like walk and drive. The Hunter she'd known a decade ago had been so strong and so capable.

He'd returned ten times stronger than he'd been as a twenty-year-old, but he was broken. Now, the man sitting beside her in the car he drove, was alive. Alert. Sure, his body might be a bit battered, but his spirit was glorious and beautiful.

"So you called my mother," he said, not really asking.

"I got her number from Mabel," she said. "And yes, I

called her. It occurred to me that I'd never apologized to them, and I needed to."

Hunter reached over and squeezed her hand quickly, but he couldn't hold it. He drove with his right hand, and Alice found one drawback of the hand controls—she couldn't hold his hand while he drove.

She wanted to put the window down and let the ocean air whip through her hair. But Hunter had said it was too cold for the beach, and he was right.

It might be mid-March and getting warmer by the day, but it certainly wasn't beach weather yet.

She told him about her communications with his parents, driving to pick them up, going to dinner with them last night. She told him everything he'd missed over the past few weeks about her job, her family, her life.

When she finally stopped talking, he said, "I'm going to do better."

"You don't need to do better," she said. "We just need to be on the same page."

"Yeah," he said. "We do." He glanced at her. "Westin's birthday is in two weeks. We should plan something for him together. I...." He cleared his throat and looked out the windshield. "I think you're so used to doing things on your own, that you might not quite know how to work with me. And I left only two days after we were married, and I know I don't quite know how to work with you."

Alice appreciated his honesty, and she knew the road before them was long, and somewhat twisted. But she didn't want to be on the journey with anyone but him. "I agree," she said. "But I'm willing to work on whatever we need to."

"Me too," he said, and Alice finally felt like they were on the same page. "So Westin seems equally excited about everything," he said. "He loves baseball, and dinosaurs, and riding bikes, and video games. What kind of party do you think he'd like?"

"We've done several things in the past," she said.

"Tell me about them," Hunter said, and Alice didn't detect an ounce of bitterness or anger in his voice, despite the fact that he'd missed all of Westin's birthdays so far. So she told him about the Minion party, the music party, the Hotwheels party.

"I didn't do a party every year," she said. "Sometimes I just made a cake and we ate at my parents. Parties are a lot of work."

"What did you do last year?"

"He had friends over, and we went to the movies," she said. "It was easy. Popcorn for everyone. Cupcakes in the park after. My house was clean."

Hunter remained quiet for a moment before saying, "I think I'd like to have a big party for him," he said. "It's my first birthday with him."

Warmth filled Alice from head to toe. "That's fine, Hunter," she said. "Maybe we can ask Mabel if the Mansion is available. We can have dinner and games and everyone can come, even pets."

"That's a great idea," he said, glancing down at his steering wheel. He pressed a button and said, "Call Aunt Mabel."

The radio silenced, and a moment later, a robotic female voice said, "Calling Aunt Mabel."

The line rang through the speakers, and Hunter said, "My car has tons of hands-free features. The military paid for them all."

"That's great," she said at the same time Mabel said, "Hunter? Why are you calling me in the middle of the day?"

He chuckled and said, "We want to have a big birthday party for Westin at the Mansion. What does March twenty-ninth look like for you?"

She grumbled something about needing to go look, and then she said, "That should be fine. I have a few appointments that day, but no events at the Mansion."

"We want to book it," he said, smiling at Alice. He kept his arm resting on his right leg, that hand pulling on a lever to keep the car moving while he used his left hand to steer. It really was amazing that he had so much of his mobility back—so much confidence. So much charisma. He was so much more like the Hunter she'd known and loved.

He continued making plans with Mabel, but Alice looked out the window and into the sunshine, closing her eyes against the bright light. She imagined that this hot, bright, calm feeling was exactly what joy felt like, what hope would be like if it became physical.

"All set," Hunter said. "I'll take care of everything."

Alice nodded, because she was finally in a place where she'd love for him to take care of everything. All the details. All the decisions.

She trusted him, and whatever he wanted to do was fine with her.

It was a very liberating feeling, and she wondered if it even came close to how Hunter felt about being able to drive.

Two weeks later, she arrived at the mansion alone. Hunter had had Westin all day for his birthday, and Alice would be lying if she hadn't experienced a bit of disappointment that morning when she'd woken to a quiet house. No balloons. No laughter or skipping around as Westin celebrated another year on the earth. No cookie dough pancakes for breakfast.

It had basically been like any other day, and she didn't like it. Her whole life had changed when Westin was born, and she remembered this day vividly—more than almost any other.

The little bundle the nurses had put in her arms came with a shock of dark hair and the softest grunting noises as his tiny body shifted. She'd fallen in love with him instantly, and his name had fallen from her lips easily.

She'd become a mother because of Westin, and she loved being his mom more than anything else.

Hunter turned toward the door as she entered, and his smile lit her whole soul. He gestured for her to come over, and she did, being careful in her sandals on the slightly uneven rock floor.

The Mansion was beautifully preserved, with its huge rock construction, sprawling staircase, and elegant ball-room. All of it had been transformed into something more kid-like and family-friendly, with dozens and dozens of brightly colored balloons on the tables in the ballroom.

There were only five of them, but they seemed to fill the whole space just fine. Westin had invited a few friends, and the rest of the guests were family members. Her parents were coming, and so were Hunter's. Mabel and her boyfriend would be there, as well as Trent and Lauren. It felt almost like a repeat of the family party Lauren had hosted on Forgotten Road, but the atmosphere here was vibrant and playful.

"Hey," he said, sweeping one arm around her waist. She'd lost count of how many times she'd come home from work to find him parked in her driveway. He always got out to greet her, always kissed her right there in the driveway before they went inside for a few minutes. Then he'd go to work and she'd go to bed.

Sometimes he'd be sitting on her couch when she got

up, and she'd learned not to go padding down the hall to make coffee without being properly dressed pretty quick. He'd kiss her then too, and tell her he loved her, and ask her questions about their son and their past life.

She realized that he had never done any of that before, and that he was ready to connect with her—and Westin— in a new way.

"This looks great," she said, still trying to take in all the streamers and the table full of presents. "Oh, I see where my gift goes." She moved over to the table and put her navy blue gift bag on it, another pang of emotion hitting her. She'd never just been one of many presents. She and Westin had always celebrated together, just the two of them.

Well, it's not just the two of you anymore, she told herself. There was room for Hunter in their lives, and she pushed against the resistance that naturally came.

"He's out back," he said. "But he wanted me to tell him right when you got here." Hunter started for the exit on the other side from where she'd come in, moving extra slow over the uneven stones.

Alice went with him, the chatter from Mabel and his mother fading with each step. Outside, the air was really warming up now that it was almost April. The first flowers on the apple orchards around town would likely be next week, with the Spring Fling the week after that.

"Westin," Hunter called, still walking toward the back corner of the Mansion. "I told him not to go too far. Clara's with him." He whistled, a loud, clear sound that seemed to echo all the way down into the valley below, where the town of Hawthorne Harbor spread out.

"It's beautiful up here," Alice said. "I'd forgotten."

Hunter turned back to her. "When we get married again, where do you want to do it?"

Surprise pulled her eyebrows up. "When we get married again?" They'd said I love you and spent a lot of time talking over the past couple of weeks. But not about marriage, and not about having more children.

"Yeah," Hunter said, his eyes taking on that dark, desire-filled look she'd seen many times before. "We're going to be a family, Alice."

"Well, I'm not wearing a ring."

"Not yet," he said with a smile as a dog barked. Clara crested the hill, her tongue hanging from her smiling mouth. She looked back and waited for Westin to appear before trotting toward Hunter.

"We were married in the summer last time," Hunter said. "I'm thinking maybe we do something different this time. Winter. Not on the beach."

"So in the mountains?"

He looked at her as Clara came to his side; Westin still had dozens of yards to come, so he couldn't overhear them. "Wherever you want, Alice," he said. "Whenever you want. I'll be there, and no one will be canceling it afterward." He stepped into her personal space and kissed her, a rough, masculine kiss that took her breath away.

Then he went inside without looking back, so that by the time Westin arrived at the corner of the Mansion, Alice was able to have her celebration with him privately. "Hey, my love," she said, bending down to hug him tight. "Oh, I missed you today. Have you had a good birthday?"

"The best, Mom," he said. "I mean, it's obviously not been the *best*. Dad didn't take me for pancakes, but we had mashed potatoes for breakfast instead. It was okay." He shrugged like he'd had a really average day.

Alice smiled at him, feeling her eyes fill with tears. "It's okay if it's been the best," she whispered. "Every year should be better and better, right?"

Westin looked into her eyes. "I love you, Mom." He hugged her again, and she wished she had his gift so they could have their special moment just like they always did.

A wet nose nudged her arm, and she twisted to see Clara there, the bag hanging from her mouth. A quick glance toward the door behind her showed Hunter going inside, and more love than Alice knew what to do with flooded her.

"Okay," she said, taking the bag from Clara's mouth gently. "You get to open my present first."

As Westin ripped the tissue paper out of the bag, she thought about what Hunter had said. *Whenever you want. Wherever you want. I'll be there.*

"Mom, no way!" Westin stuck his hand in the bag and pulled out the personal game machine. "You said I couldn't have one." His eyes looked like they were lit from inside, and she smiled.

"Yeah, well, you're getting older, and if you can follow the rules, then it should be okay."

"What rules?" he asked, turning the box over.

"I'm not sure yet," she said. "Your dad and I need to talk about them. Then we can both enforce them, no matter who's house you're at."

Westin threw his arms around her, and she hugged him back, the birthday moment she'd craved all day. "Love you, bud."

He pulled away, much more sober now than she'd ever seen him on his birthday. She stroked his hair off his forehead. "What's wrong, Westin?"

"Are you and Dad going to ever live in the same house again?" He looked up at her, those clear, dark Magleby eyes so innocent. So hopeful.

She straightened, her knees starting to hurt from the crouched position. She took Westin's hand and started for the door where she'd last seen Hunter. "Yeah," she said. "We will. We just need to get married first."

With that, Westin cheered, pumped his fist, and ran for the door, calling, "Dad! Dad, come see what Mom got me!"

Hunter sped down the Coastal highway, the Pacific Ocean on his right and his window down to let in the sea breeze. He loved the temperature on the water in July, and he loved that he and Alice were taking Westin to the beach.

She'd confessed to him that she'd avoided the beach since he'd left, and that made his heart sad. But he'd done similar things—cutting specific items out of his life if they reminded him too much of her.

But they didn't have to do that anymore. Now, they were building a life and family together, day by day, brick by brick.

It had not been easy over the past few months. He'd done things that had upset her. She'd done things that had upset him. But they were committed, and Hunter felt more and more foolish every day that he'd thought he and Alice could've made their first marriage work.

Something stewed inside him, and he decided now was a great time to bring it up with Alice. The sun shone, the ocean was blue, there wasn't a care in the world.

But there was inside Hunter.

"I think I need to go talk to your parents," he said, drawing her sunglassed attention toward him.

"Why?"

"Because." He shrugged, but this wasn't casual. "I think your mom was right when she said we were too young to get married last time, and I just ignored her. I probably should talk to her."

"If you want to, Hunter," Alice said. "But I think they're okay with us now."

"Yeah." He knew they were. But he also knew they'd probably blamed him for a lot of things, and that his reappearance in town months ago had once again cost them something dear—time with their grandson.

He let the subject drop, because they were almost to the beach, and he had to focus on the task at hand.

Asking Alice to marry him.

The first time he'd proposed in the park where so many of their memories had been made. Meeting there the summer after high school before they went their separate ways. They'd reconnected at the Spring Fling in April the next year, and they were married before July dawned that same year.

So fast.

Everything had happened so quickly back then. It felt like life or death.

But now, Hunter had been taking things slower. Part of that was because he'd learned how to slow down in the Marines, and his body forced him to do certain things slower now too. And no matter what, he did not want to hurt the nine-year-old boy in the backseat if he took things too quickly.

He turned into the parking lot, and they obviously weren't the only ones to think a day-trip to the beach sounded like a good idea on this sunny day. "All right," he said. "I'll get the umbrella. Westin, you get the cooler and your backpack. Clara, you stay by me."

"I'll get the chairs," Alice said, getting out of the car and reaching back in for her beach bag. She already wore her suit, her coverup billowing in the breeze.

Hunter liked this beach because it had a sidewalk that went pretty far down toward the water, and he'd have a flat, hard surface to walk on for most of the way. He'd already asked Alice to help him the rest of the way, and she and Westin went ahead of him to stake out their spot, while Clara plodded along slowly beside him.

He watched her set up their chairs in the sand, a rush of love flowing through him at how much she did for him. A lot of burdens had been eased when he'd gotten his car, but she still continued to be at his side, day in and day out, no matter what he needed. And he loved her so much for it.

She claimed she liked having him at her side too, but he wasn't sure he did much for her. Inadequacy plagued him, but he pushed it away. Alice had never said or done anything to make him think he wasn't good enough for her, and he would fight this mental demon until it died.

He paused and checked his pocket for the diamond ring. It was still there, hard against his leg. He adjusted the umbrella over his shoulder and touched his cane again. "All right, Clara," he said. "We just have to make it across the sand to the chairs."

"Hey, do you need help?" a man asked, and Hunter's first instinct was to say no to the man who was probably five or six years younger than him. He patted Clara, who's eyes drifted closed in bliss and smiled at Hunter.

Instead of rejecting the offer, Hunter nodded, and said, "Yeah, my family is just right there. My girlfriend will come help, but we could get started." There was no shame in accepting help. He'd learned that lesson in the six months he'd been back in Hawthorne Harbor too.

The young man took the bulky umbrella from Hunter and looped his arm through Hunter's right one, steadying him on that side further. "What happened, man? Accident or something?" He nodded to the scars on Hunter's shoulder and neck, visible because of the tank top he wore.

"War happened," he said. "I served in the Marines for almost ten years."

"Oh, wow." He moved carefully but with strength and surety Hunter would never have on the sand. "I'm sorry about that."

"Me too," Hunter said. "But hey, I'm still alive." He caught Alice's eye as she looked back to find him, and alarm crossed her face. He waved at her that he was fine, because he was. He let the twenty-something deliver him to his family, and he said, "Thanks so much."

"Thank you," he said, backing up a few steps before running through the loose sand and back to his friends.

Alice stared at him long enough for Hunter to go, "What? He offered to help."

"And you took it."

"Yeah." Hunter sighed back into his chair. "I took it."

"Mom, can I go in?" Westin asked.

"Yes," Alice said at the same time Hunter said, "Wait a minute."

Westin looked back and forth between them, and Alice looked at him too. "So I had a question real quick," he said, his mouth suddenly so dry. And he should've asked that guy to help him set up the umbrella too. It was pretty breezy today, and it would need to be pounded down into the sand to get it to stay.

He dug into his pocket and pulled out the ring, keeping it concealed in his fist. "I love you, Alice. And I love you, Westin. And I want you to both live with me in the cabin full-time. No more dropping off and picking up and going back and forth."

Hunter opened his fist and showed them both the ring. Alice sucked in a breath and her eyes widened. Westin grinned and started hopping around in the sand like it was too hot to stand in one place.

"Will you marry me?"

Alice sat very still, her eyes glued to the diamond in his hand.

"Mo-om," Westin whined. "Why are you just sitting there?"

She looked at their son and back to Hunter, tears gathering in her eyes. "Yes," she whispered.

A grin split Hunter's face, and he leaned forward to kiss her. Westin cheered while they shared an engaged kiss, and then Hunter slipped the ring on her finger.

"I'm not sure what you did with the last ring," he said. "But I think it's good to have a fresh start."

"I still have it," she said.

"Would you rather wear that?"

Alice gazed down at her hand, a look of admiration in her eyes. She'd looked at her previous ring like this too, even though that diamond had been pitiful and the best he could afford. But he could do better now.

"No," she said slowly. "I love this one, and we do need a fresh start."

"Maybe you could make a necklace out of the first one or something."

"We'll see," she said. "Do you still have your wedding band?"

"Yes," Hunter said, his voice turning to the past a bit. "It's in my jewelry box."

"Would you like a new one?"

He reached over and took her hand in his. "I just want you."

Alice smiled, and she looked so, so happy. "Go on, Westie. You can go now."

Instead of skipping down the sand to the surf, he launched himself at Alice and Hunter and hugged them. "I love you," he said. "When are you going to get married?"

He was tired of going back and forth, Hunter knew. He'd asked his son about it, and Westin had told him.

"That's up to Mom," Hunter said.

"First week of January," Alice said without much hesitation.

Hunter glanced at her. "Yeah? Why's that special?"

"That's when you returned to town," she said, meeting his eye. "Returned to us."

He pressed his lips to her temple, happiness coursed through him. "Six more months, bud. We can do it."

"Okay," Westin said, bending to pick up a shovel. "I'm going to go build a sandcastle."

"All right," Alice said as he walked away. She leaned her head against Hunter's shoulder and nodded toward their son. "Do you want more kids?"

"Definitely," Hunter said, hoping he could make it six more months without Alice in his house, in his bed.

"Me too," Alice said, letting her eyes drift closed. "Me too."

SIX MONTHS LATER:

Hunter couldn't believe he was getting married in the hospital chapel. It had maybe 8 benches for people to sit on, and they were all full. They'd been selective in who they'd invited to the ceremony, and yet, forty people had squeezed into the tiny room with the big stained-glass window above the altar.

Alice's family wasn't huge, but she'd invited her nurse friends from the children's wing, and a few of her single mom friends.

In another thirty minutes, she wouldn't b a single mom anymore. He wouldn't be a single dad. They'd have one house to live in, two cars, and a hedgehog and a dog all under one roof.

Hunter couldn't wait.

He stood at the altar in his full Marine uniform, his eyes trained on the doors only about twenty feet away. Last time, she'd walked down a long aisle barefoot in the sand, and her parents hadn't even been there.

Today, they sat in the front row, and Hunter couldn't believe this was the second chance they were all getting.

He had gone to talk to Karen and Christopher, and they'd tearfully accepted his apology for the follies of his youth.

And now, he was ready to start his life with the woman he loved and their son.

Finally, Westin appeared in the doorway, and Hunter's pulse kicked into a new gear. His son looked to his right and gestured for someone to hurry up, which caused the audience to giggle and twitter.

And then Alice joined Westin, linking her fingers through his. She wore a beautiful white dress that was radically different from the one she'd worn a decade ago. This one was long and simple, with lace covering almost the whole thing. Her hair was loose and wavy over her shoulders, and she carried an elegant bouquet of pink roses.

Her smile landed on Hunter, and he grinned back at her.

She and Westin proceeded down the aisle, and then Westin moved to stand beside Hunter. The pastor—a man who worked right there at the hospital—started talking, and just like last time, Hunter didn't really hear much of what he said.

At least he was short-winded, and it seemed like only seconds before he pronounced Hunter and Alice man and wife.

"You may kiss your bride."

Hunter tipped Alice back amidst cheering and kissed her, his wonderful, beautiful wife—for the second time.

He couldn't hold her that way for long, as his right leg started to tremble.

"No cancelations," he whispered against her lips.

"No," she agreed. "That's not happening."

He righted her and lifted their joined hands before taking his cane and starting down the aisle. "Come on, bud. Let's get this party started."

Last time, they'd had a huge reception at the Magleby Mansion. This time, they went down the street to The Bluebird, a restaurant that served classic American fare and had one of the oldest operating ice cream counters in the state. They'd rented the banquet room, and they shared a meal with their family and friends.

Then he got behind the wheel of his car, his wife in the passenger seat, and his son in the backseat. As people cheered and blew bubbles, he backed out and turned onto the street that would lead them to the highway out of town.

"Well, we did it," Alice said, a giggle following her words. She still wore her wedding dress, but she had a suitcase in the trunk.

"Yeah," Hunter said, taking his left hand off the steering wheel to loosen his tie. He met Westin's eye in the rearview mirror and then looked at Alice. "I love you guys."

"I love you too," they chorused back, and Hunter's joy exceeded anything he'd felt before. What a year it had been. What a wild, wonderful year it had been.

Hawthorne Harbor
SECOND CHANCE ROMANCE
the end

David Reddington couldn't wait to get back to shore. The ocean wind felt like ice against the exposed parts of his face, and as one of the eight civilians who worked at the Port Angeles Station, he had the next three days off.

Away from the station. Away from the politics of border control and immigration and boarding boats to make sure everyone had the proper paperwork. What he really needed was a good deep sea rescue—not that he wanted anyone's life to be in danger.

Most of all, Dave just didn't want to be bored while on-board the ship he captained for the Coast Guard. A mental chuckle moved through him. *Bored on-board. Bored on-board.*

But the fact was, Dave had just turned forty, and every-thing about his life was boring.

"You watching the game tonight?"

Dave turned toward Ben Erwich and smiled. "Yeah," he said. "Wouldn't miss it."

"You could come over," Ben said, pushing his dark hair off his forehead before putting his hat back on. "Me and a couple of the guys are going in for pizza and drinks."

Dave thought about it for a second. He'd been invited to football games before, but he'd never gone. "I can't tonight," he said, making a quick decision. He was the captain of Adelie, and he wanted to keep that professional barrier between him and the crew.

It was flexible, and practically transparent, but it was still there.

"You should host it," Ben said with a grin, because he knew how much Dave hated having people over to his house. "I know my place is too small for you."

"It is not," Dave said, though the apartment Ben got with his housing allowance was pretty pitiful. Dave supposed not everyone could get permission to live twenty-five minutes away, in the town where they grew up, in a house just down the street from their parents.

But Dave had worked for over two decades for the United States Coast Guard, and he wasn't going to feel bad that he'd put in for an assignment closer to his parents and Hawthorne Harbor so he could feel like he had a home.

When he'd first started in the Guard, he'd lived on a ship, for crying out loud. He'd earned all of his honors and privileges, and he wasn't going to feel bad about them. Port Angeles didn't have barracks, so the men and women right out of basic training had no idea what it was like to live in cramped quarters and never have one single second to themselves.

True, some shared apartments, but Ben didn't.

Dave leaned against the railing, the scent of salt and seaweed sharp in his nose. "I have to record the game anyway," he said. "So no group texting where you talk about every play."

"What do you have going on tonight?"

He exhaled, but the heavy sound of it got whipped away by the wind. "Oh, there's a town meeting tonight for the Spring Fling. I'm seriously considering skipping it." He'd grown up attending the Spring Fling every April, and warmth filled him at the thought of going again this year.

He'd been back in Hawthorne Harbor for four years after a long time away, and the town festivals and traditions held just as much magic and spirit as they had when he was a kid. The Spring Fling was all about apples, and blossoms, and romance—surprisingly. But it wasn't even January yet, and the first planning meeting had been set for the event, because there were a lot of activities to coordinate.

From a bachelor auction, to a dance, to a bake-off, to guided tours of the apple orchards, someone had to make sure tourists and townspeople alike had the time of their lives come the third weekend in April.

And he knew who that someone was—Mitch Magleby. The Magleby's had their fingers in every pot on Hawthorne Harbor, but Mitch ran the community center's outreach program, and they funded and organized the Spring Fling. The community center also hosted the Festival of Trees, so Mitch was always seen around that as well.

Dave didn't care about Mitch all that much—but Mitch's daughter.... His pulse thumped erratically just thinking about Brooklynn.

And Dave had learned last year that Brooklynn volunteered on the Spring Fling committee. So maybe he'd signed up to help too. Maybe. Maybe not.

He still wasn't sure if he was even going to go to the meeting.

He let the boat and the crew on her distract him, and the time back to land passed quickly. Dave had a multitude of things to check, and lists to go through, so he began the docking prep while his seamen, petty officers, and ensigns completed their tasks and left the ship with bags over their shoulders.

They'd only been out for a couple of days, so Dave would have no problem transitioning from sea to land—at least physically.

Mentally and emotionally though, he loved the ocean. The gentle way it rocked him to sleep at night or waved hello during the day. He loved the tang of it in his mouth, and he could never figure out how humans stayed on land and worked for a living.

He felt sure he was a water creature, as it had always called to him. He'd left for the Coast Guard basic training the day after he graduated from high school, and he'd never looked back. The Guard had been a good career for him, and he'd worked his way up to Captain and gotten a post close to his family, all of whom still lived in Hawthorne Harbor.

Retirement crossed his mind again as he went through his last checklist. He could retire now and get his pension immediately. Maybe then he wouldn't be bored.

He scoffed at his thoughts. "What would you do with yourself?" he muttered under his breath. "You think you're bored now." He shook his head, finished his work, and went to his office. Now, when he had to sleep on the boat, he had his own quarters. He could handle small spaces; it was just the constant crowds that had gotten to him as an entry-level officer in the Guard all those years ago.

He joined the other men and women calling goodbye to each other, catching sight of a woman leaning against his SUV down on the end of the row. "It holds itself up," he called to Audrey Lynn, a helicopter pilot for one of the three rescue copters they had at the station.

She grinned at him as he approached. "You're done for the weekend, aren't you?" she asked.

"Yeah." Though it was only Thursday, Dave didn't have

to be back until Monday morning. And even then, it was just to check on a fishery and do some environmental protection around the hook of the inlet. "You're on all weekend, aren't you?" He opened the back door and put his backpack inside.

"She'll be there tonight," Audrey said, lifting her phone and showing him the screen.

"You asked her?" A groan started way down in his toes even as he scanned Audrey's text conversation with Brooklynn. So she'd confirmed she'd be there. He frowned at Audrey. "I'm not fourteen."

"No, that sorry gut of yours says you're forty and haven't been on a date in years."

"She won't say yes." Dave unlocked the SUV and held out the keys. "Did you want to drive?"

"Heavens, no," Audrey said, moving around the front of the vehicle to get in the passenger side. She lived in Hawthorne Harbor too, and they often carpooled if possible. Out to save the environment and all that. Plus, Audrey didn't exactly have a reliable ride.

He hoped she'd drop Brooklynn as a viable subject of conversation, but he knew better. If he didn't want to talk about his old crush on a woman would wouldn't go out with him, he'd have to ask Audrey something that would keep her talking for twenty-five minutes.

"I heard you got a new pilot," he said as he twisted the key in the ignition. "And he's somewhat of a playboy."

"Oh, please," Audrey said with an eyeroll attached.

"You should hear the women in the office talk about him. He's so handsome and so tall." She scoffed as if being handsome and tall were crimes against humanity. "All I care about is if he can hold the bird steady while people thrash around in the ocean."

"Right," Dave said, because he wasn't the only one who was single and hadn't been out with anyone in a while. "So why don't you go out with him? Get to know him better? Welcome him to Port Angeles?"

Audrey gave him a wide-eyes, horrified look. "Why would I do that?"

"Why wouldn't you?" He turned onto the highway, his plan working.

"I am the *senior* flight officer here," she said, glaring now. "I can't believe you would even *suggest* I should do such a thing." She huffed and tossed her shoulder-length hair over her shoulder. "Besides, he's like ten years younger than me."

Dave burst out laughing, because that sentence alone testified that Audrey wanted to go out with her new pilot. She wouldn't. But she wanted to.

And she spent the next twenty-five minutes detailing why she wouldn't, and defending herself that she didn't even want to.

THAT EVENING, DAVE CHECKED THE CLOCK EVERY FIVE minutes. At least it felt like he did. He needed fifteen minutes to get to the community center, and at six-forty-five, he didn't leave the house. Nor at six-fifty.

He could arrive fashionably late. It was a small town—was anyone on time?

He left his house at six-fifty-five, and he arrived at the community center to find the parking lot almost full. "What is going on here tonight?" he asked himself. He really needed a dog so when he got caught talking to himself, he could at least say he was chatting with the pooch.

A family hurried toward the entrance, their son carrying a basketball with him. Ah, rec game night. No wonder he had to park way in the back of the lot and walk through the weather to get inside.

"Uh, I'm here for the Spring Fling planning meeting?" he asked the woman at the front desk, and she directed him around the corner and down the hall. His steps grew more and more timid the closer he got. He didn't want to be the only one in the meeting.

He wasn't concerned about being late, but a tremor of anxiety hit him when he heard someone talking into a microphone just inside the appointed room. Pausing in the doorway, he scanned for two things: a place to sit and Brooklynn Perrish.

There were plenty of places to sit, as the room was about half-full. He spotted Brooklynn's blonde hair over on the left side, in the third or fourth row. She had seats on both sides of her. So while the woman up front continued to talk about the upcoming festival, Dave started toward the outside edge of the rows. No need to go right down the middle and call attention to himself.

He kept his eyes trained on Brooklynn, so much so that he wasn't watching where he was going. His foot caught on the leg of one of the metal folding chairs, sending it crashing into the one next to it.

He grabbed onto the backs of two chairs to steady himself, making more noise and drawing everyone's gaze to him. The woman up front stopped speaking.

"Hey," he said, lifting one hand when he realized he wasn't going to face-plant it right there on the carpeted floor. "Just a little late."

He rounded the corner and hurried forward, stepping over the man and woman on the end of Brooklynn's row. "Sorry," he said. "Sorry, can I get by? Sorry."

Chairs scraped as people moved, and Brooklynn's face turned a shade of pink that made Dave's heartbeat accelerate too. She was gorgeous with all those curls spilling over her shoulders, and while she shielded her eyes from him, he knew what color they were.

A deep, dark green, like the depths of the ocean when he got past the surface.

He half-sat, half-stumbled into the seat next to her, actually bumping her with his shoulder. "Sorry," he said again, looking up front. The woman had continued, but Dave had certainly made a splashy entrance.

"Hey, Brooklynn," he whispered, leaning down so his mouth was closer to her ear. "What did I miss?"

"Are you kidding me right now?" she hissed. "What are you even doing here?"

Brooklynn Perrish felt the weight of every eye as they continued to dart over to where David Reddington had sat down beside her. Practically on top of her, the oaf.

Even as she thought it, she regretted it. He was definitely not an oaf, and the scent of his cologne muddied her thoughts enough to mute Alecia's voice at the front of the room. When Dave was nearby, he consumed all her mental energy.

And she really hated that.

"I came to volunteer for the Spring Fling," he said in a whisper. "Isn't that why you're here?"

Yes, it was. Well, one of the reasons. Why couldn't Ginny face the front? There was nothing to see back here in the fourth row. Nothing, if Dave didn't count as the most eligible bachelor in town.

And to Brooklynn, he didn't. Oh, no, he did not.

She didn't want another relationship, especially with Dave. Surely he knew that. He'd asked her out enough times and she'd told him no over and over.

Thankfully, he didn't ask now, and Ginny finally turned all the way back to face Alecia, who was still going on about the activities the committee had planned. As if Hawthorne Harbor hadn't been hosting the Spring Fling for ninety-two years now.

She looked down at her lap, where she'd balanced a notebook before Dave had come in and interrupted everything. Yes, she'd helped organize different parts of the Fling for years now. Why did she need to take notes?

She had no idea, only that she had. Her fingers twitched, and she started scribbling furiously to catch up on what she'd missed.

Dave sat there, unconcerned about notes. He seemed to be listening, but he could've just as easily been daydreaming about fishing or whatever he did on that huge boat out at the port.

Brooklynn once again felt a tug of regret. She knew what he did on *Adelie*, and it wasn't fishing. She wasn't sure why she was so antagonistic toward him.

Oh, wait. Yes, she did.

He loved the ocean. Went out on a boat every dang day.

And that same ocean had stolen her husband from her. Snatched him from the sky and snuffed his life out.

And that rescue boat Dave manned just down the coast? Couldn't rescue Ryker.

Anger built inside her, giving way quickly to sadness and misery. When someone raised their hand to ask a question, she grew impatient. She really couldn't sit here and smell Dave's cologne all night, listening to idiotic queries about if the date could be changed.

Of course it couldn't. The Spring Fling was always the third Saturday of April. Always. The apple trees were guaranteed to bloom by then, and that was a huge part of the festival. Plus, everyone had survived tax season, and the Spring Fling had originated in town by the local accounting office at the time. Her great-grandfather had owned that firm, and the tradition had been born.

And that brought her to another reason she was seated in the fourth row of this freezing room on a January night when she'd rather be baking.

She was a Magleby, and Magleby's were expected to be involved around town. After all, her parents hadn't left town like a few others, and just because she'd been married for eight months and bore a different last name on her driver's license, she was still a Magleby, still in town, and thus, still expected to volunteer.

So she sat up straight and kept her pen moving across the page as Alecia talked. She finally finished with, "There are sheets up here to sign up for the different activities. We need as many people as we can get." She stepped away from the microphone, and the silence in the room broke as people got up and started forward.

Chatter broke out, and Brooklynn looked at Dave.

Big mistake.

For he was so handsome—*gorgeous!* her mind screamed—and she hadn't seen him in a few weeks. So she really needed a few seconds to drink in those dark, dreamy eyes, the slope of his straight nose, that strong jaw that never had a beard.

He must shave three times a day, she thought, glancing up to see his hair was getting long.

And by long, she could probably pinch it between her fingers if she tried. But she wasn't going to do that. Oh, no, she was not.

She blinked when he smiled and nodded behind her. "Do you want to go sign up?"

No, she didn't. "Yes," she said, getting to her feet. Her back groaned, as she'd had a fifty-pound dog in the grooming van that day. Her website said the limit was forty pounds, but she was a sucker and couldn't say no to a customer. Especially Nellie Ridgeway.

"You okay?" Dave asked, and Brooklynn looked back at him.

"Yes, why?"

"You seemed like you...never mind."

She pulled her hand away from her lower back, where she'd been pushing to relieve some of the ache there. She didn't need to hobble around in front of him like she was Aunt Mabel's age.

Brooklynn put some distance between them, glad when he engaged in another conversation with someone else. In fact, she lost track of Dave entirely a few minutes later, and she wondered if he'd shown up to volunteer or just sit by her.

Warmth filled her from sole to scalp, because while she hadn't accepted any of his invitations, the fact that he asked her out was flattering.

Brooklynn just wasn't sure she could ever love someone as much as she'd loved Ryker. Not only that, she didn't even go to the beach anymore. How could she be with Dave, a man whose job required him to go out on the ocean?

No, she couldn't. It was easier to reject him than to even imagine that they could be together.

She signed her name to several papers and left the community center. If she hurried home, she'd still have time to make those caramel mocha brownies. And maybe, just maybe, the sweets would quell some of the anxiety in her gut that had been plaguing her since Ryker's death three years ago.

THE NEXT MORNING, BROOKLYNN PULLED IN TO THE ANIMAL shelter, the plate of brownies beside her almost distracting her from the familiar SUV already in the lot.

She knew this car....

Brooklynn's fingers tightened around the wheel. She had an appointment with a corgi in twenty minutes, and she was just stopping by for a moment. Just to give Laci the brownies. Her sister had just broken up with her long-time boyfriend, and she'd texted Brooklynn that she might not survive the day if she didn't have chocolate.

So Brooklynn had plated up the cookies and left without putting makeup on. It didn't matter. Her canine customers didn't care what she looked like when she groomed them. The sky threatened to open up and dump rain on Hawthorne Harbor today anyway, and Brooklynn was considering canceling her appointments if the clients didn't have a garage or something she could use.

She normally didn't mind working out of the back of a van, but sometimes it got stuffy in there, and she almost always stood outside. But not in the rain.

"It'll take two seconds," she told herself, wondering why in the world Dave was at the animal shelter. She probably wouldn't see him anyway, as her sister worked with the vets in a separate part of the building than the adoption center.

After grabbing the brownies, she headed for the door, not enthused by the drumming of thunder overhead when she touched the door handle.

Inside, the building felt much too bright compared to outside, and she glanced to her left, expecting to see Laci standing there in her pale pink scrubs. Instead, her eyes met Dave's.

"Hey," he said, his smile warming his whole face as he stood. Surprise laced the three-letter-word. "What are you doing here?"

"My sister works here," she said, lifting the plate of brownies. Why was her heart tapping around like that? How did she make it stop? Didn't it know Brooklynn had sworn off men?

Fine, it tapped out. But Dave is a captain. Not just any old man.

He was older than her, something she actually liked. He had silver coming in around his ears, and if he kept smiling at her with those white teeth, she'd be going out with him that weekend.

"What are you doing here?" she asked, reaching for her phone in her purse and navigating on it so she wouldn't have to look at Dave's handsome face.

Gorgeous, her brain reminded her.

"Oh, I'm taking a dog for the weekend."

She lifted her eyes to his, finding him downright adorable with the way he tucked his hands in his back pockets. "A dog for the weekend?"

"Yeah, they let you take them for a few days," he said. "Get them out of here. I think they think I'll finally adopt one." He chuckled.

"So you do this a lot."

"Yeah," he said evasively.

"And you don't want a dog full-time?"

"I do, yes," he said. "I love dogs. But my job isn't very conducive to having a pet. I have to sleep on the boat sometimes."

Horror snaked right through her, leaving a cold, wet trail in its wake. "That sounds terrible," she said at the same time her brain put *dog lover* in the pro column for Dave. Why it kept reminding her how wonderful and good-looking he was, she wasn't sure.

He cocked his head and studied her with those eyes that could undo all of her defenses. Her phone buzzed, and she flinched as she looked at it.

"Laci's coming out."

"How's she doing?" he asked.

"She just broke up with her boyfriend," Brooklynn said. "Thus, the brownies."

"Is that why you made brownies?" Dave asked, just enough interest in his voice to know his question wasn't casual.

"No," Brooklynn said. "I don't date, Dave."

"Just checking." He looked toward the door Laci came through, smiling at her too.

"Dave," she said with surprise. It was no surprise that Laci knew who he was. They'd all grown up together in Hawthorne Harbor, and Brooklynn had certainly spilled many of her traitorous secrets to Laci in the middle of the night.

Laci looked from Dave to Brooklynn, and then gave him a quick hug. "It's good to see you. Are you adopting?"

"No."

"So you're following Brooklynn now." She cocked her hip and folded her arms, glaring at the man she'd just hugged.

Brooklynn wanted to crawl in a hole and curl into a ball. "Lace," she said at the same time Dave started laughing. How he could make such a joyful noise, she wasn't sure. Brooklynn hadn't felt that level of happiness in a long, long time.

Thirty-six months.

Three years.

Over one thousand days.

"No," Dave said again, still chuckling. "Though I'd love to go out with her. I know when a woman's not interested." His eyes flicked to hers for a moment. There, then gone. He ducked his head, a hint of a blush entering his face, before turning and going over to the counter.

"Here," Brooklynn said, thrusting the plate of brownies toward her sister. "That was so embarrassing. Why'd you say that?"

Laci took the plate. "I don't know. He hasn't asked you out again?"

She watched him take the leash from the adoption aide. "Not for a couple of months." She didn't mean the words to come out coated in so much sadness. Regret lanced through her. What if he never asked her out again?

He turned toward them, the light in his eyes dimming when he saw them still standing there. He took the mutt around the couch away from them, saluting her with, "I'll see you in the morning."

He'd almost moved out the doors when Brooklynn's mouth caught up to her brain. "Wait. What's in the morning?"

"The planning meeting for the bachelor auction," he said. "I guess we signed up for the same thing." And with that, he walked out, his dog for the weekend in tow.

Dave couldn't help stopping by the bakery in the morning on his way to the community center. Brooklynn liked to bake, he knew that. She always had. She'd had a birthday party when she turned thirteen, and it had been at the community college kitchens. Everyone had participated, and though Dave's brother's cake had been wet in the middle, it had still tasted good.

When they'd gone to their junior and senior proms together, she'd baked cookies each time. He could still smell them as he drove in his car, though this was a vastly different vehicle than what he'd driven in high school.

They hadn't had a real romance in high school. Not by his standards. They'd gone out a few times, and he'd kissed her twice. But the call of the ocean had been stronger than waiting in town for two years for her to finish high school, and Dave had left. In fact, nothing had ever called as strongly as the Coast Guard, a ship, or being out on the water.

Until now.

Now, his bones ached a bit more in the morning. Now, he wondered why he didn't retire and just teach water safety classes to kids on the weekends in the summer. None of this going out on the ocean in the winter stuff. No sleeping on ships. Or dealing with men twenty years younger than him who thought they knew more than him.

He pulled a peanut butter bar out of the bag and took a bite, the rich chocolate frosting mixing with the sweet and salty bar. A moan started in the back of his throat.

This morning, the parking lot was just as full as last night. People going in and out in exercise clothes, earbuds in, told him that the New Year's resolutions had quite worn off yet. "Give it another month," he said to himself as he parked.

He'd been up since five, and the six miles he'd put in on the beach were history. He loved running on the beach as the day woke up, though he couldn't get himself to go later in the winter and ended up running in the dark for months.

He had a headlamp and this morning, he'd had Valkerie, the cute pit bull mix he'd picked up the previous morning. She'd run and run and run, and if Dave was going to get a dog, he wanted one that could run as far as he did.

But he wasn't going to get a dog, even if it would curb his loneliness at night.

Inside the community center, he went past the front desk with, "I'm here for the Spring Fling meeting." The woman seated there barely looked up, and this time, Dave wasn't late. In fact, the only person in the room was Brooklynn Perrish.

His stomach tightened at the sight of her, of all that blonde hair he wanted to rake his fingers through. "Morning," he said, his voice perfectly pleasant and not giving away any of the raging hormones in his forty-year-old body.

"Good morning." She smiled at him, more than she'd done in the last six months.

He took the seat next to her and held out the bag. "I stopped and got you something."

"You did?" Her eyebrows went up and she looked at the bag and then him before taking it from him. The smile returned as she peered inside. "A peach bearclaw. These are my favorite." She removed the pastry from the bag and took a bite. "Mm."

Dave's whole body heated up so fast it was like someone had doused him with gasoline and tossed a lit match at his feet. "They're better in the summer, but Jean says she uses frozen peaches from last summer during the winter." Why was he talking about peaches?

"I love them," she said. "I haven't had one in a while. Thank you." She touched his hand, and a zing of electricity shot up his arm. Their eyes met, and for once, she didn't look away. And she didn't look frustrated or guarded either.

As Dave gazed at her, he realized he was seeing the real her. The one she kept hidden behind notebooks and brownies and rejections.

"Maybe—" he started just as someone said, "There you are. We're meeting in room two-oh-two. Come on."

Brooklynn broke the spell between them by looking away. "Oh, I didn't realize." She jumped to her feet and started down the aisle toward the exit.

Dave sat there and tried to get his pulse to return to normal. He couldn't believe he was four words away from asking her out. Again.

Had he not learned anything from the previous half a dozen times he'd asked and she'd said no?

She didn't date. He knew that. And yet, the invitation had been right there, so willing to come out.

He also knew *why* she didn't date, and he'd been hoping that three years would be long enough for her to move past the death of her first husband. Heck, it would be four years in June.

But Dave had no idea what it felt like to lose a loved one in a freak accident, and he couldn't judge her. Couldn't push her.

He also didn't need to open himself up to get his heart shredded, and as he got to his feet, he told himself, "You will not ask her out. You will not," over and over again as he followed her and the woman who'd interrupted him to the right room for the meeting.

Entering last again, he found himself in a room full of women, each with a notebook like Brooklynn's. His heart sank to the bottom of his boots, but he pulled up a chair to the round table, his knee practically touching Brooklynn's.

"Okay," a woman said. "Let's go around an introduce ourselves. I know most of you." Her eyes landed on Dave, and no, he didn't know her.

"I'll start," he said. "I'm Dave Reddington. I work for the Coast Guard."

The ladies went around, and he managed to remember Delaney and Michelle before the names started to blur. Delaney had almost black hair that had to come from a bottle, and she ran the meeting. He'd be fine if he could remember her name.

They talked about a theme for the bachelor auction, and it was decided that "Spring for your Fling" would be the tagline for the event. While Dave sort of hated it, all the women seemed excited about it, even Brooklynn. Honestly, the only way he'd be excited about the bachelor auction at all was if they had dozens of boxes of pizza there, and there was the possibility of eating it with Brooklynn.

"So now we need men," Delaney said, her pen poised to write. The woman on her left started naming names, and Dave could barely keep up.

When the Talker paused, Brooklynn said, "Let's add Dave to the list."

"What?" he almost shouted, horrified as Delaney started writing his name. "No, let's not add Dave to the list."

Brooklynn looked at him, her eyes wide. "Why not?"

"Why would I want to do that?"

"It's for a good cause."

"Is it? The community center does need new carpet, but come on." He nodded to Delaney's paper. "That's not my thing."

"It's just an interest list," Brooklynn said.

"I'm not interested."

Delaney and the other women switched their gazes to Brooklynn, anticipating her next argument. Dave felt a swarm of bees gathering in his chest, but he was ready to die on this hill. He would not parade in front of the single women of Hawthorne Harbor and hope one of them would bid on him. Not happening.

"What about for a maybe?" Brooklynn asked.

A growl started in the back of his throat. "*Maybe* I'll have to work that day."

"You don't work the weekends."

"Sometimes I do." Dave folded his arms, and he'd be blind if he didn't notice that all the women glanced down at his biceps and back to his eyes. "Let's move on."

"This is the last thing," Delaney said. "Then we'll split up the list and make contact with the men. We need at least twenty, you guys. Last year, we only had eleven, and it wasn't enough."

Dave wanted to say that perhaps the lack of men willing to be bid on said something. Maybe they shouldn't be doing this event as part of the Spring Fling.

"We'll just need to make it really fun this year," Michelle said, and that was another maybe Dave hadn't considered. He had no idea how it would ever be fun for a man to go out on stage and hope someone found him attractive enough to pay to go out with him.

Dave already had plenty of pressure in his life, thank you very much.

"These are your men." Delaney slid a list with five hand-printed names on it.

"I have to ask other men to do this?" He wasn't even sure how to do that.

"Which is why it would be better if you did it too," Brooklynn said with just a bit of bite in her voice. "Then you can tell them how much fun it will be and how things will work." She gave him a cocked-eyebrow *so-there* look.

He wanted to throw her sass right back in her face and then take her to lunch. Neither of those were going to happen, so he remained silent. He practically smashed his list in his fist and got up. "Are we done?"

"Yes," Delaney said. "Can you meet next Saturday?"

Dave really wanted to say no, but he nodded instead as the other women gave their assent.

"Good," Delaney said. "Try to talk to as many men as

you can this week. Then we'll have a better idea of where we are for next week."

Dave turned to leave, even Brooklynn's presence not as comforting as he usually found it. After all, she was the one trying to get him to do the auction. Why? So he could fetch the lowest amount? Or not be bid on at all? What was her goal in making him put his name on the list?

It didn't matter. He drove home in the pouring rain to Valkerie, who sat in front of the window and watched the water flow down. "Sorry, girl," he said to her as he kicked his feet up on the ottoman in front of him. "Maybe it'll clear up and we can throw a ball in the backyard."

Hours later, the weather hadn't cleared at all. In fact, it seemed like Mother Nature had parked her storm clouds right over Hawthorne Harbor and had no plans to move them. He'd watched more football and basketball games than anyone should watch in one day, and he was *bored*.

Until his phone chimed out a message from Brooklynn.

His heart caught somewhere in his throat, making breathing and reading difficult.

Hey, so I have a big favor to ask you.

A favor? He could barely type, and he had to go back and fix the word *favor* like four times before it was right.

Yeah, she messaged back. *There's this bachelor auction for the Spring Fling, and you'd be perfect for it.*

He frowned at his phone. "Who does she think she's

talking to?" She surely had his number. He'd called and texted her before lots of times. Too many times, in fact.

I might be willing to break my no-dating rule if you'll do it.

Dave's breath went right out of his body. "Oh, she's not playing nice," he said, but his lips curved up into a smile. He hated texting when he could call, so he pressed the phone button and lifted his device to his ear.

Brooklynn expected Dave to call, but when her phone buzzed in her hand, it still startled her. And sent another wave of electricity up into her shoulder, same as when she'd touched his arm.

Why had she done that?

Why had she sent that text?

I might be willing to break my no-dating rule if you'll do it.

That was it; she'd lost her mind.

Cinnamon barked as if to say *someone's calling you,* and Brooklyn flinched again. Her fingers fumbled over the screen, but she managed to tap the green phone icon and connect the call. "Hey," she said.

"Are you serious?" he asked, his voice still in the lower range of growly. Brooklynn had actually never seen Dave when he wasn't chipper and upbeat, and to see him get all hot under the collar about not doing the bachelor auction had practically sent her to the hospital for heart palpitations.

"Because it's not very fair to yank me around like that," he said. "I don't think it's a secret that I—"

"I'm serious," she blurted out. What she really was, was tired. Oh, so tired of trying to resist him. A corner of her heart wailed, something about Ryker and how Brooklynn couldn't be unfaithful to him.

She silenced it and straightened her back though she was alone and Dave couldn't see her. Just the thought of going out with him had her brain bouncing around, and she didn't think there was any possible way she could sleep tonight.

"When would you like to go?" he asked, his voice gentle now.

She tried to speak and ended up coughing. Why was this so hard? She was thirty-eight-years-old and had been out with plenty of men. Heck, she'd been engaged and then married. It seemed unfair that Dave Reddington made her so nervous.

Of course, she'd been on the anxious side since Ryker's death. Her mother had pushed her to go to therapy, but Brooklynn hadn't wanted to talk about the accident or her feelings or any of it.

She'd already had her little westie, and she'd simply added two more dogs to her home in an attempt to feel less lonely. Less upset. Less panicky about every little thing.

"Brooklynn?" Dave asked. "Did I lose you?"

"I'm here," she said. "Sorry, I'm...thinking."

"Okay, so I'm at work this next week, obviously. But I'm not scheduled to be on the boat overnight. I'm usually home by six or so, and we could go to dinner. Or you can wait until next weekend, and we'll go to breakfast or something."

Brooklynn didn't want to wait until next weekend, a thought that surprised her. Honestly, she'd put Dave off for the past year, and there he was, calling the moment she'd gave him any hint she might be interested.

It wasn't a secret that he was, that much was true.

"What about tomorrow?" she asked.

"Tomorrow?" he repeated, heavy shock in the word.

"Yeah," she said. "The lodge up at Olympic Park has a great brunch buffet."

"Yeah, sure," he said, a smile in the words. She imagined it lit up on his face, and with a date looming less than twenty-four hours away, Brooklynn knew she'd get no rest that night. "I'll pick you up at nine?"

"See you then," she said, and the call ended.

"Oh, my stars," she breathed, falling backward on her bed. Cinnamon, the little shorkie who had yipped at her to answer the phone came over and started licking her hand. Brooklynn stroked her with it, and that brought the other two dogs over too.

Cory, the white westie she'd had for seven years, flopped down partially on her chest, pushing her breath out of her lungs as if reminding her to breathe. "Hey, bud," she said, patting him. He was square, like a little ottoman, and she'd loved him from the very first moment she'd seen him.

She also had a yorkie named Callie, and she curled up near Brooklynn's head. "We're not sleeping here, guys," she told them. But she did love how they'd all rallied around her, almost like her girlfriends would in high school after she'd called a boy.

Not that Brooklynn ever called boys in high school. Oh, no. She wasn't painfully shy, but she certainly didn't need any extra attention on her. She'd been on the swim team, and she'd done well. Didn't break any records. Didn't win every time. But the recognition she got from her parents and her coach was enough.

"Come on," she told the dogs as she pushed Cory off her chest and sat up. "We need to figure out what to wear to brunch." And to do that, she'd need to enlist the help of a woman who'd actually been out with a man recently.

"Jules," she said when her best friend answered. "It's a code pink."

Julie gasped and then shrieked. The sound cut off suddenly and was followed by, "You better not be kidding me right now."

"I'm not. I'm going out with Dave Reddington tomorrow morning for brunch up at the park. So get over here. I'm freaking out."

Julie giggled and said, "I'm on my way," and Brooklynn

flopped back onto the bed. And maybe, just maybe, a giggle escaped from her mouth too.

"Okay, so the blue sweater is really nice," Julie said, walking around Brooklynn and tugging on the orange sweater she now wore. "But this one is perfect."

"You don't think it says fall?" Brooklynn asked, looking at herself in the mirror. A burnt orange color, the sweater was cute. It had larger looping that the blue one, and it slid off her shoulder on the right every so often, which she actually liked. "I look like a pumpkin."

"Honey, you do not look anything like a pumpkin." Julie brushed one more imaginary piece of link off Brooklynn's arm. "It's awesome. This is the one. And with those black jeans?" She purred. "He's not going to be able to keep his hands to himself."

"But I want him to keep his hands to himself."

Julie scoffed and waved her hand. "You do not. Or you wouldn't have called me." She gave Brooklynn a quick glare in the mirror. "Now, jewelry. Then we'll talk about makeup." Julie was in her element, and Brooklynn loved being with her when she got into date mode.

Brooklynn simply liked being with another human being on Saturday night. After Ryker died, she'd been so isolated, assuring everyone she was fine to get them to leave her alone. But then, she was left alone, and there were some days when she couldn't handle the pressing silence. The meals for one. Walking past the pictures of the two of them and the life they were supposed to have, and now didn't.

"I think something simple with jewelry," Julie said. "Silver to accent the rustic orange. These long teardrops are nice." She held up a pair of earrings Brooklynn had forgotten she owned. After all, the pups she spent her days with didn't care what dangled from her ears.

She nodded, and Julie handed them to her. "You're not going to wear the ring, are you?"

Brooklynn shook her head, tears springing to her eyes quickly.

"Oh, honey." Julie wrapped her arms around Brooklynn, holding her together. "It's been a long time, but are you sure you're ready for this?"

Brooklynn took a few seconds to push her emotions back down her throat. "I am, Jules." She took a deep breath. "I have to be."

"And you like Dave, right?" Julie stood back and held Brooklynn's shoulders at arm's length. "Because if I could get that man to even glance my way, I'd steal him from you. He is gorgeous, and funny, and rich."

Brooklynn pushed out a quick laugh, though he was all of those things.

"But he only has eyes for you," Julie said. "Trust me, I've tried to get him to look my way." She retreated back to the dresser while Brooklynn put in her earrings.

"I don't know how you moved on after Jim."

"Well, Jim didn't die," Julie said. "We didn't get along for a long time before the marriage ended. So it's different."

Fear struck her between the ribs. "I haven't been out with anyone in a long time," she said. "What do I even talk about? What do I do?"

Julie handed her a necklace with two hearts joined together. "Let's try this." She moved behind Brooklynn, who gathered up her copious amount of hair and held it while Julie worked the clasp on the necklace.

"First off," she said. "You don't worry so much. It's not as hard as you think. You know Dave. You like Dave. So you talk to Dave and get to know him better. That's it."

"What if he holds my hand?"

"Girl, enjoy it." Julie finished with the necklace. "And if he doesn't hold your hand, I'd be shocked."

Brooklynn looked at her hands, wondering how it would feel to have someone hold her hand. She hadn't held hands with a man in years.

"Oh, and you eat." She nodded toward the bathroom. "Let's go for a more dramatic look with the makeup since we're playing nice with the jewelry."

"I don't like how the necklace lays," Brooklynn said, fiddling with the hearts. Julie had given her this necklace after Ryker had died. "It's not right with the neck on the sweater."

"You're right. No necklace." Julie removed it and

ushered Brooklynn into the bathroom. "Dave has a brother who's married. And a nephew. Ask him about them. Ask him about his crew. Ask him about the dog he got the other day. There are all kinds of things to talk about."

Maybe for Julie. Brooklynn felt blank most of the time, and she hated it. She felt like life had turned black and white the day Ryker had died, and she existed in a comic strip. She stood there in the little box, a conversation bubble above her head, waiting for someone to come fill in what she should say, what she should think.

"Eyes closed," Julie said, and Brooklynn complied.

"You'll come over in the morning and do my makeup, right?" Brooklynn asked.

"Honey, I brought my pillow," Julie said with a laugh. "That guest bed is still made. I peeked in there when I got here."

Brooklynn smiled, a rush of gratitude and love filling her. "Thanks, Jules." She opened her eyes and looked at her best friend. "Thank you so much."

"Of course." Julie picked up the neutral palette and a makeup brush. "Now let's see what we can do."

THE NEXT MORNING, BROOKLYNN WORE THE TIGHT BLACK jeans. The orange sweater. The long, sliver teardrop earrings. The bronze and gold and glittery makeup. Julie had spent forty minutes with a flat iron and Brooklynn's hair, making sure every piece curled and waved just right.

"You are beautiful," she said with a hug only moments before the clock would strike nine. "Inside and out. And remember, he already knows it. So own it."

"Love you," Brooklynn whispered to her friend. Jules sniffed and tucked her dark hair behind her ear.

"I need to find me a man like Dave. He has a younger brother. Maybe Joey's available."

"You'd go out with a fishmonger?" Brooklynn asked.

"Have I ever been picky about who I go out with?" Julie asked with a smile.

It was true. She wasn't picky. She'd been in a couple of serious relationships since her divorce five years ago, but nothing had stuck. And she wasn't hopeless. She wasn't depressed. She didn't stay home with her three dogs and bake her anxiety into pies, cakes, and breads.

Brooklynn drew in a deep breath and paced over to the front door. Peering through the peephole, she didn't see him. "He's late."

"It's one minute after," Julie said. When Brooklynn turned around, she found her friend shaking her head and smiling as she poured herself a cup of coffee. She'd made it that morning, so it would probably taste good. Brooklynn could put flour, sugar, and chocolate together into delicious combinations, but making good coffee? She simply didn't know how to do it.

The doorbell rang, which sent all three dogs to

barking and Brooklynn's heart to pounding. She still stood at the door, only inches from Dave on the other side of it.

Julie said something, scooped up one little yapping dog, and disappeared down the hall. Brooklynn's pulse boomed in her ears, and she couldn't believe she was about to go out with another man.

And not just any man.

Dave Reddington.

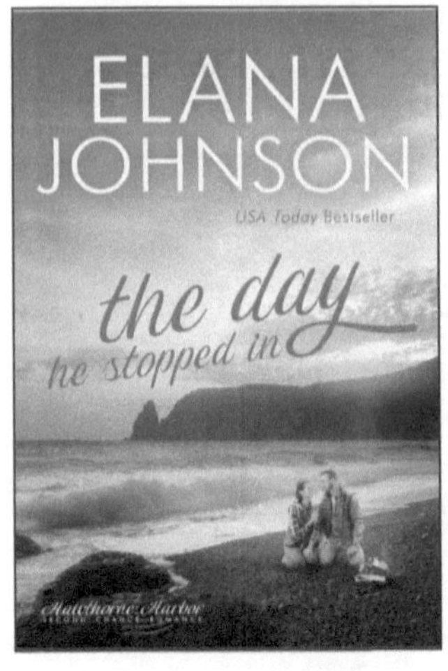

The Day He Stopped In (Hawthorne Harbor Second Chance Romance, Book 2): Janey Germaine is tired of entertaining tourists in Olympic National Park all day and trying to keep her twelve-year-old son occupied at night. When longtime friend and the Chief of Police, Adam Herrin, offers to take the boy on a ride-along one fall evening, Janey starts to see him in a different light. Do they have the courage to take their relationship out of the friend zone?

The Day He Said Hello (Hawthorne Harbor Second Chance Romance, Book 3): Bennett Patterson is content with his boring firefighting job and his big great dane...until he comes face-toface with his high school girlfriend, Jennie Zimmerman, who swore she'd never return to Hawthorne Harbor. Can they rekindle their old flame? Or will their opposite personalities keep them apart?

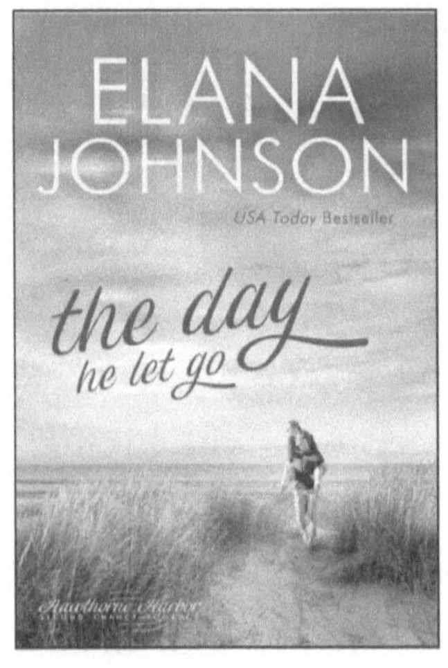

The Day He Let Go (Hawthorne Harbor Second Chance Romance, Book 4): Trent Baker is ready for another relationship, and he's hopeful he can find someone who wants him and to be a mother to his son. Lauren Michaels runs her own general contract company, and she's never thought she has a maternal bone in her body. But when she gets a second chance with the handsome K9 cop who blew her off when she first came to town, she can't say no... Can Trent and Lauren make their differences into strengths and build a family?

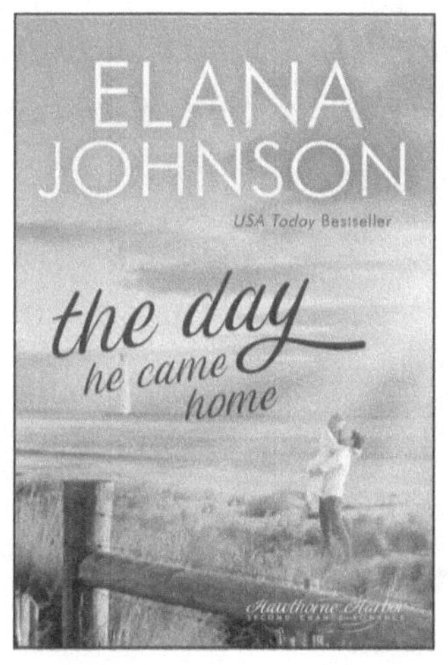

The Day He Came Home (Hawthorne Harbor Second Chance Romance, Book 5): A wounded Marine returns to Hawthorne Harbor years after the woman he was married to for exactly one week before she got an annulment...and then a baby nine months later. Can Hunter and Alice make a family out of past heartache?

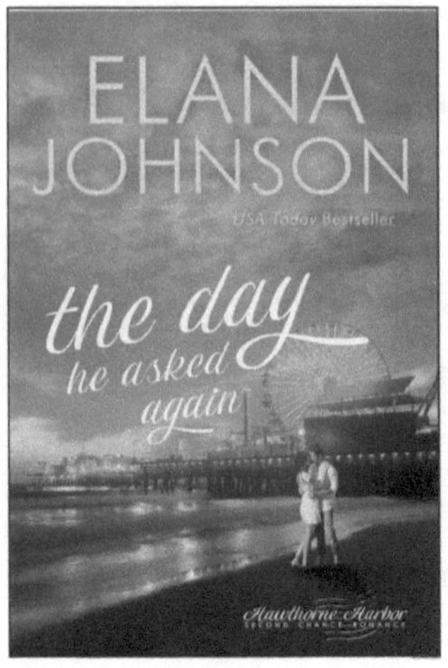

The Day He Asked Again (Hawthorne Harbor Second Chance Romance, Book 6): A Coast Guard captain would rather spend his time on the sea...unless he's with the woman he's been crushing on for months. Can Brooklynn and Dave make their second chance stick?

The Billionaire's Driver (Book 2): A car service owner who's been driving the billionaire pineapple plantation owner for years finally gives him a birthday gift that opens his eyes to see her, the woman who's literally been right in front of him all this time. Can he open his heart to the possibility of true love?

The Billionaire's Fake Engagement (Book 3): A former poker player turned beach bum billionaire needs a date to a hospital gala, so he asks the beach yoga instructor his dog can't seem to stay away from. At the event, they get "engaged" to deter her former boyfriend from pursuing her. Can he move his fake fiancée into a real relationship?

The Billionaire's Cinderella (Book 4): The owner of a beach-side drink stand has taken more bad advice from rich men than humanly possible, which requires her to take a second job cleaning the home of a billionaire and global diamond mine owner. Can she put aside her preconceptions about rich men and make a relationship with him work?

The Billionaire's Bodyguard (Book 5): Women can be rich too...and this female billionaire can usually take care of herself just fine, thank you very much. But she has no defense against her past...or the gorgeous man she hires to protect her from it. He's her bodyguard, not her boyfriend. Will she be able to keep those two B-words separate or will she take her second chance to get her tropical happily-ever-after?

The Billionaire's Boyfriend (Book 6): Can a closet organizer fit herself into a single father's hectic life? Or will this female billionaire choose work over love...again?

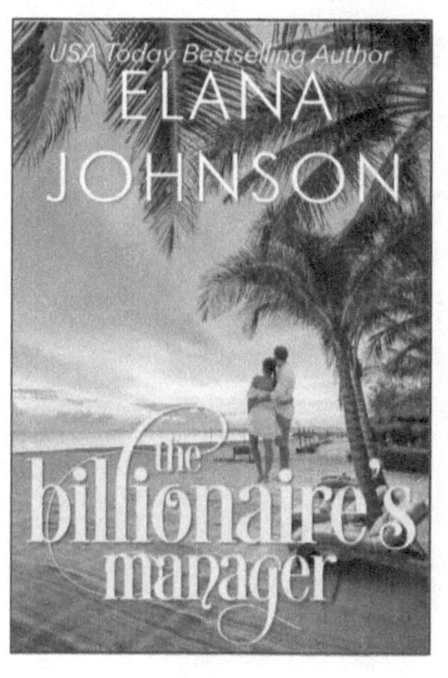

The Billionaire's Manager (Book 7): A billionaire who has a love affair with his job, his new bank manager, and how they bravely navigate the island of Getaway Bay...and their own ideas about each other.

The Billionaire's Ex-Wife (Book 8): A silver fox, a dating app, and the mistaken identity that brings this billionaire faceto-face with his ex-wife...

The Helicopter Pilot's Bride (Book 1): Charlotte Madsen's whole world came crashing down six months ago with the words, "I met someone else." Her marriage of eleven years dissolved, and she left one island on the east coast for the island of Getaway Bay. She was not expecting a tall, handsome man to be flat on his back under the kitchen sink when she arrives at the supposedly abandoned house. But former Air Force pilot, Dawson Dane, has a charming devil-may-care personality, and Charlotte could use some happiness in her life.

Can Charlotte navigate the healing process to find love again?

The Billionaire's Bride (Book 2): Two best friends, their hasty agreement, and the fake engagement that has the island of Getaway Bay in a tailspin...

The Prince's Bride (Book 3): She's a synchronized swimmer looking to make some extra cash. He's a prince in hiding. When they meet in the "empty" mansion she's supposed to be housesitting, sparks fly. Can Noah and Zara stop arguing long enough to realize their feelings for each other might be romantic?

The Doctor's Bride (Book 4): A doctor, a wedding planner, and a flat tire... Can Shannon and Jeremiah make a love connection when they work next door to each other?

The Rockstar's Bride (Book 5): Riley finds a watch and contacts the owner, only to learn he's the lead singer and guitarist for a hugely popular band. Evan is only on the island of Getaway Bay for a friend's wedding, but he's intrigued by the gorgeous woman who returns his watch. Can they make a relationship work when they're from two different worlds?

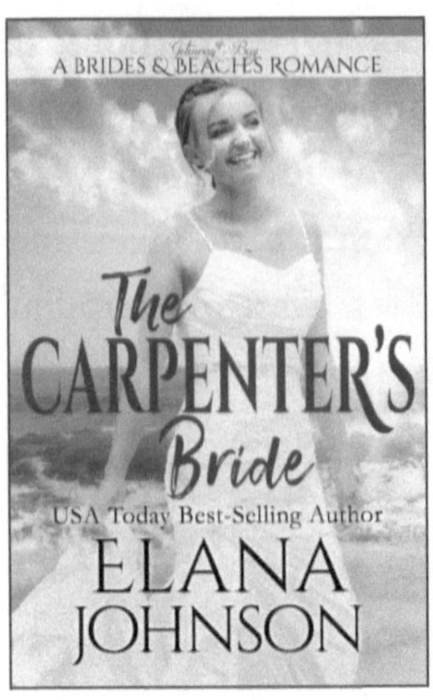

The Carpenter's Bride (Book 6): A wedding planner and the carpenter who's lost his wife... Can Lisa and Cal navigate the mishaps of a relationship in order to find themselves standing at the altar?

The Police Chief's Bride (Book 7): The Chief of Police and a woman with a restraining order against her... Can Wyatt and Deirdre try for their second chance at love? Or will their pasts keep them apart forever?

Kisses and Killer Whales (Book 2): Friends who ditch her. A pod of killer whales. A limping cruise ship. All reasons Iris finds herself stranded on an deserted island with the handsome Navy SEAL...

Storms and Sentiments (Book 3): He can throw a precision pass, but he's dead in the water in matters of the heart...

Crushes and Cowboys (Book 4): Tired of the dating scene, a cowboy billionaire puts up an Internet ad to find a woman to come out to a deserted island with him to see if they can make a love connection...

Accidental Sweetheart (Book 2): She's excited to have a neighbor across the hall. He's got secrets he can never tell her. Will Olympia find a way to leave her past where it belongs so she can have a future with Chet?

Bodyguard not Boyfriend (Book 3): She's got a stalker. He's got a loud bark. Can Sheryl tame her bodyguard into a boyfriend?

Not Her Real Fiancé (Book 4): He needs a reason not to go out with a journalist. She'd like a guaranteed date for the summer. They don't get along, so keeping Brad in the not-her-real-fiancé category should be easy for Celeste. Totally easy.

She Loves Him...Not (Book 5): They've been out before, and now they work in the same kitchen at The Heartwood Inn. Gwen isn't interested in getting anything filleted but fish, because Teagan's broken her heart before... Can Teagan and Gwen manage their professional relationship without letting feelings get in the way?

ABOUT ELANA

Elana Johnson is the USA Today bestselling author of dozens of clean and wholesome contemporary romance novels. She lives in Utah, where she mothers two fur babies, taxis her daughter to theater several times a week, and eats a lot of Ferrero Rocher while writing. Find her on her website at elanajohnson.com.